I0450768

A CANYON ROAD CHRISTMAS

THE WITCHES OF CANYON ROAD:
BOOK FOUR

CHRISTINE POPE

This is a work of fiction. Names, characters, places, and incidents are either the product of the author's imagination or are used fictitiously. Any resemblance to actual events, places, organizations, or persons, whether living or dead, is entirely coincidental.

A CANYON ROAD CHRISTMAS

ISBN: 978-1-946435-18-7

Copyright © 2018 by Christine Pope

Published by Dark Valentine Press

Cover design by Lou Harper

Ebook formatting by Indie Author Services

All rights reserved. No part of this book may be reproduced in any form or by any electronic or mechanical means, including information storage and retrieval systems—except in the case of brief quotations embodied in critical articles or reviews—without permission in writing from its publisher, Dark Valentine Press.

Don't miss out on any of Christine's new releases—sign up for her newsletter today!

1

Miranda McAllister-Castillo

Rafe set his phone down on the kitchen table and said, "The bishop can squeeze us in on Friday the twenty-third."

I leaned against the back of the hard chair where I sat and gazed across the table at Rafe, at his coffee-brown eyes and the heavy lock of black hair that always fell forward onto his forehead no matter what he did to force it to behave. As much as I loved looking at him, I wasn't feeling as excited by the news he'd just delivered as I knew I probably should be.

Did I really want our wedding to be "squeezed in" anywhere? It felt as if the entire month that had just passed had been a squeeze in and of itself, thanks to moving into the enormous old hacienda-style mansion that had been the home of the Castillo *primas* for generations, and helping Rafe's father Eduardo relocate to Rafe's house, which was located less than a quarter-mile away. My father-in-law seemed settled enough now, although I wished we could have persuaded him to stay with us for just a bit longer. However, he insisted that Rafe and I should be able to settle into our new lives on our own, and not be forced to share the house with anyone.

Frankly, I didn't feel as though I was being forced. Eduardo had been my father-in-law for only a month, and I already loved him as though he was my own father...although I had to admit that I couldn't think of two men who were more different. But Eduardo brushed aside our protests and moved his things to Rafe's former home—and set about refurnishing it and having some of the rooms repainted. Already it felt far more homey than it had when it was Rafe's bachelor pad, mostly because Rafe didn't care about interior decorating and tended to choose items because of their usefulness, and not because they were aesthetically pleasing. As much as that particular quality might exasperate me sometimes, I had to admit that it did keep the arguments about my own redecorating of the *prima*'s house to a minimum.

Not that I'd done a lot of that yet. I was still

trying to get used to my new role as *prima* of this clan, although I hadn't really been called upon to do anything more earthshaking than preside over the christening of the newest Castillo, Rafe's cousin Arthur and his wife Casey's daughter, named Maria Genoveva in honor of Rafe's late mother. I'd felt nervous enough performing that minor task, mostly because I hadn't been raised Catholic and only had the foggiest idea of what was going on.

To be honest, I'd kind of been hoping that everyone would let Rafe's and my sketchy courthouse wedding slide, and that we could go on with our lives without getting embroiled in all the preparations that a big ceremony at the cathedral involved. Unfortunately, the older generation—aided and abetted by Rafe's Aunt Rosa —put their foot down and said we must have a real wedding. They might have been deprived of being able to attend their *prima's* funeral…at the time, Rafe and I had both thought it was too dangerous to have a large gathering like that, with the dark warlock Simon Escobar still on the loose and all too willing to take advantage of such a tempting target…but they were not going to let their new *prima* avoid a big wedding ceremony at Loretto Chapel.

Which was why Rafe had been on the phone with the bishop, trying to find an opening for us during one of the church's busiest seasons. I probably should have been grateful that he could fit us in at all, but right then I felt more tired than anything else, and possibly a little apprehensive. After all, even though Simon was dead and no longer capable of casting dark spells that could confuse the mind and cause a person to utter the dreadful words Rafe had said to me while we stood at the altar, I couldn't quite push aside the niggling fear that something else might go wrong this time as well. We were already married, and as far as I was concerned, something that wasn't broken didn't need any fixing.

That argument wouldn't wash with Aunt Rosa and the rest of the Castillos, unfortunately, so here we were.

"Okay," I said wearily, knowing there was no point in wasting any energy on protests. "Sounds like Cat and I need to go dress shopping."

If Tess Diaz, the woman who owned the wedding boutique, wondered why I was back at her shop to purchase another gown only a little more than a month since I'd bought the last one, she didn't give any sign of it. By that time, most of the people who lived and worked in the heart of Santa Fe knew of Genoveva's passing, even if the circumstances of her death had to be hidden from the civilian—nonmagical—sector of the population. Her obituary said she had died of a brain aneurysm, which, for all I knew, was no more than the truth. Of course, that explanation left out the small detail of that aneurysm being caused by a dark warlock's even darker spell, but we couldn't exactly go spreading that news around town.

No doubt some gossip had filtered through the community about the big wedding at Loretto Chapel that ended in disaster, but I'd already determined to stonewall my way through this if necessary. Luckily, it seemed that Tess was more interested in staying on the Castillos' good side than she was picking my brain about my first abortive wedding ceremony, because after getting some sparkling water for Cat and me, she excused herself to go pull some dresses for me.

"Hopefully, different ones than what I tried on last time," I murmured to my sister-in-law Cat as we sat on a pair of elegant velvet-upholstered side chairs. "Because I got the only one I really liked from that bunch, and it's long gone."

Well, to be fair, the dress wasn't exactly gone forever. I just couldn't bring myself to go back to the house on Cienega Creek where Simon had taken me after I'd agreed to go with him in order to prevent any further violence, but several senior

Castillo witches and warlocks had gone there so they could sweep the place of Simon's belongings —and remove his body, which now lay in an unmarked grave in a corner of Rosario Cemetery. I hadn't asked where that grave was; I really didn't want to know.

Anyway, in addition to Simon's clothes and other effects, they found my first wedding dress, which had been in my bags when I ran away from Rafe after the first horrible ceremony at Loretto Chapel, but had disappeared somewhere along the way. Now I knew where it had been—hanging in the closet of the house where Simon had been holding me, cleaned and pressed, as if it was waiting for another chance to be worn. Had Simon kept the dress because he thought he would convince me one day to marry him? That seemed the most plausible explanation, even if it was enough to give me shivers even now.

"I'm sure Tess will come up with something," Cat replied, not looking terribly concerned about the situation.

Maybe she was thinking we only had to find something that would be passable, that didn't have to be held up to her mother's exacting standards. I supposed that was true enough, but I still wanted to look beautiful for Rafe. I didn't want him to think I was half-assing this thing because I'd been pressured into it by the family. Besides, this wedding ceremony would include my relatives as well, since we no longer had Genoveva handing down her ridiculous edicts, including insisting that no McAllisters or Wilcoxes attend my wedding to her son. Now that I knew I had family coming, it only made sense that I would want to look my best for everyone.

While Cat probably would never have admitted it, I guessed that some—if not most—of her current relaxed state had something to do with not having her mother around to nag her night and day anymore. She did look far more serene than I'd yet seen her, a calmness to her big dark eyes that I hadn't observed before, her lovely features untroubled by a frown. No one could say that Cat didn't love Genoveva, but the former *prima* had been a very domineering person. At last Cat was free to make her own choices, first of which was moving out of the big house where she'd grown up and into a luxurious vacation rental only a few blocks away. How she'd managed to land that place when pretty much everything in the downtown area had already been booked for the holidays, I didn't know. Maybe some of her father's magical talent for having things always go his way had rubbed off on her.

Tess came back into the dressing area, towing a rack of gowns behind her. Although white dresses tended to blend into each other, especially when all hanging in a row like that, it didn't seem as though any of the ones she'd brought out were repeats of the gowns I'd tried on the last time I was in the shop.

That was somewhat encouraging, even though climbing in and out of a series of wedding dresses was not normally the way I preferred to spend my afternoons. Still, since I had already agreed to this whole enterprise, there wasn't much I could do except go ahead and get this over with as soon as possible.

Possibly because we'd already been through this once before, it did seem as though Tess had done a better job of dialing in my preferences. She knew I liked embroidery but wasn't a fan of too much frou-frou, and that while I was all right with something strapless, I didn't want something with a mermaid-style silhouette. Even so, I tried on and rejected three gowns before I knew I'd found the one.

It was silk organza, with an elegantly draped bodice and bead and crystal ornaments at the shoulders and the waist. That was it for decoration, but the dress really didn't need anything more than that, because the way it fit was so perfect, you'd have thought it had been custom made for me, instead of something I was buying off the rack.

"Oh, wow," Cat said as I stood on the little

dais in front of a bank of mirrors, turning this way and that, listening to the soft whisper of the silk fabric. "That is really stunning."

"It just came in a few days ago," Tess informed us. "So you wouldn't have had a chance to try it on the first time you were in." She seemed to realize she'd slipped into dangerous territory, because she went on hastily, "That is…it's a new line."

"It's fine, Tess," I said. "I know the circumstances are a little unusual." She still looked a bit discomfited at her gaffe, and so I added, "The dress is beautiful. I don't think I need to try on anything else."

"And a veil and tiara?" she asked.

"No tiara," I replied firmly. I'd already gone down that road, and I still had all-too-vivid memories of sitting in the Airbnb vacation rental Simon had passed off as his apartment and turning the tiara from my first wedding over and over in my hands, wondering what the hell had gone wrong between Rafe and me. "And no veil, either."

"Seriously?" Cat put in. "You are getting married in Loretto Chapel, you know. Aren't you going to feel underdressed?"

"No," I replied. "It's going to feel strange enough anyway, considering Rafe and I are already legally married. I'll have an updo and some crystal pins in my hair or something. It'll still look nice."

"Oh, I'm sure it will," she said. "But you know how Aunt Rosa is."

"I can deal with Rosa." My tone sounded firm and confident, although privately I wondered exactly what I would do if Rosa really decided to get into it with me about showing the proper respect for the chapel and the ceremony itself.

"Mm-hmm," Cat responded. She didn't say anything else, though, probably because she knew it wasn't a very good idea to be airing too much Castillo dirty laundry in front of a civilian.

Tess, who'd probably seen more than a few family tiffs during her time in the wedding business, said in the most neutral of tones, "I'll go ahead and get the gown rung up, then. It doesn't need any alterations, so you can take it home with you today."

"Perfect." I smiled at her and disappeared behind the decorative screen in the corner of the room so I could get back into my street clothes—just jeans and a jacket and boots, since I no longer had to worry about trying to impress Genoveva Castillo. Selfish as the thought might be, I knew that deep down I was grateful that Rafe and I could face our future together without having to deal with her interference.

The dress turned out to be just a hair under

ten thousand dollars, once the sales tax was added in. I had no idea how much my first wedding gown had cost, since of course Genoveva had handled that transaction. Even though I knew that amount of money was a mere drop in the bucket compared to the Castillo clan's wealth, I couldn't quite ignore the dry feeling in my mouth as I handed over my shiny new platinum Visa card. Ten grand was a hell of a lot of money for something I'd wear for maybe five hours, tops.

Well, I'd make sure the dress was stored carefully, and maybe someday my own daughter would wear it for her wedding. Would that future daughter also become *prima* of the Castillos one day? I really couldn't say for sure. Maybe if my powers were passed on to her, and if people were willing to wait for that day. There wasn't any real hard and fast rule about when a *prima* selected her *prima*-in-waiting; although the conventional wisdom was to choose someone fairly early on so there wasn't a lot of time when the *prima* didn't have any backup, so to speak, it didn't always happen that way. My own mother went without a *prima*-in-waiting for years because there wasn't anyone in the clan strong enough to take on that role, and I heard it was a relief to everyone when my older sister Emily began to show her powers early on, making it clear who the McAllisters' next head witch should be.

Whether or not the Castillos would be that accommodating, I didn't know. Then again, they of all people should recognize the hazards of choosing a *prima*-in-waiting just because of tradition, and not because she was really the right person to take on that role. I was only *prima* because Rafe's oldest sister Louisa had realized she wasn't up to the task of defeating Simon Escobar, and so had passed her powers on to me. None of us—myself included—wanted a repeat of that scenario.

I took the wedding gown in its designer garment bag, thanked Tess, and went with Cat to get into her Mercedes SUV. Sooner or later, I'd need to get a car for myself, I supposed, but there hadn't been a lot of time available for those ordinary sorts of tasks. I'd already had to waste the greater part of a day at the New Mexico motor vehicle department getting a new license, and that was enough to last me for a while. Maybe after the first of the year, Rafe and I could go car shopping. Right now, I just wanted to get past the one-two punch of this wedding and the holidays.

As she started the car, Cat said, her tone both shy and excited, "I think I found a place."

"You did?" I shifted in my seat so I could see her expression better. She wore a half-smile, but there was also something almost nervous about the way she engaged the vehicle's auto-drive, how she kept looking around even though the Mercedes' computer automatically swept the immediate area for any other vehicles or for people suddenly crossing into the street before it would let the vehicle start moving. "Why didn't you say something?"

"The text came in while you were trying on dresses," she explained.

"So…what is it?"

I knew that Cat didn't want to stay in Santa Fe, that she'd been looking for someplace out in the countryside where she could have some land of her own. What she intended to do with it, I had no idea; she certainly wasn't a farmer or even a hyper-enthusiastic gardener. Her main vocation —aside from being a Castillo witch—was as a fiber artist, specializing in intricate tapestries that incorporated many different types of materials. She sold her work in local shops and had won quite a few awards, but that kind of experience still didn't exactly prepare her for living off the land.

"It's the old Luna Rio winery," she said as the SUV pulled out from the curb and began to take us back toward the house that was now mine and Rafe's. "Up in Pojoaque. Dad heard about them closing from one of his suppliers. I guess the owners decided they didn't want to be in the wine business any longer, and so they're selling."

"You don't know anything about winemaking," I pointed out.

She grinned—a genuine grin this time, nothing hesitant about it. "I know. I'm not planning on making wine. I just want the property. The current vineyard manager wants to stay on, but what I can do is sell the grapes to other local wineries rather than try to make wine of my own. That way, the property can still be self-sustaining."

"It sounds like you've thought about it a lot," I said.

"I guess I have, even though I only heard about the possibility of buying the place a few days ago. I put out some feelers to the owners, and they're willing to deal. When they texted, they were asking if I was free to come out tomorrow and take a look around, maybe make them an offer." Cat glanced over at me, a hopeful light in her dark eyes. "Would you and Rafe come with me?"

"Sure," I said immediately. As far as I knew, Rafe didn't have any plans for the day, since he'd finished the last of his freelance pre-visualization commissions not quite a week earlier and had decided not to take on any new ones until after the first of the year. "I'd love to see the place."

Even as I spoke, though, I couldn't help but feel a twinge of sadness. It had been fun to have Cat so close by, to have her as well as Rafe to help me navigate the sometimes complicated familial relationships in the Castillo witch clan. If she bought this vineyard up in Pojoaque, she wouldn't be right around the corner any longer. True, she'd only be twenty-five minutes away at the most, but that wasn't quite the same thing. Still, I knew this was what she wanted, and I certainly wasn't going to stand in the way of her happiness.

I had to hope Rafe would feel the same way.

2

Rafe Castillo

IT WOULD HAVE BEEN NICE IF HE COULD HAVE shot down this idea of Cat's. Of course she was her own person and free to do as she liked—at least, she was now that Genoveva wasn't around to issue edicts—but at the same time, Rafe wished his sister had found someplace just a little closer to Santa Fe. During the drive to Pojoaque, he'd hoped the property would exhibit enough obvious flaws that it would be simple to tell her this wasn't the one, and that she needed to keep looking. But....

"It's beautiful," he said as they stood outside the main house and surveyed the grounds. The vines were dormant at this time of year, of course, looking more like carefully pruned bundles of twigs, and the ancient centuries-old cottonwoods that ringed the property were likewise bare. Even so, there was a sense of peace and beauty here he couldn't ignore. The winter sunlight slanted across the stone walkway that led from the house to a long, low outbuilding a few yards away, and the air was fresh and cool.

He and Miranda and Cat had been given the luxury of inspecting the vineyard without the owners standing by and watching, since they'd texted Cat the codes to the electronic gate that guarded the property, along with the codes to locks in the main house and the building that had been the tasting room. Looking at it now, Rafe asked, "What are you going to do with the tasting room? Throw wild parties?"

His sister lifted an eyebrow at him. "No. The owners have already sold off most of their inventory, and they said they'll throw in what's left as part of the sale of the property. I'll store the wine in the cellar—it's located under the tasting room. Then I figured I'd take out the fixtures and either sell them off or donate them, and turn the place into my fiber studio. I'll finally have the room to set up that seventy-two-inch Countermarche loom I've been eyeing for years."

"Well, it sounds like you have a plan already," Rafe said. Personally, he thought the tasting room would make a great party space, but Cat had always been serious about her weaving, and he guessed she was just itching to be able to spread out and really flex her muscle, so to speak. "You want to look at the house?"

"Absolutely."

She set off along the path that led to the main house, while he and Miranda followed a few paces behind. As they walked, Miranda's hand stole into his, warm despite the chilly December breeze, and Rafe felt himself grow a little warmer at her touch. It felt so damn good to hold her hand like this, to know she was there next to him. She didn't speak, though, but remained quiet, looking around her with interest.

There was a lot to look at, actually. Besides the house and the tasting room, there were several more outbuildings, probably where some of the actual winemaking had taken place. He supposed one of them could be converted into a garage, and the other maybe a gardening shed or something like that. With everything dead and waiting for the return of spring, it was hard to tell, but he thought he spied some raised beds for vegetable gardening off to one side, and at the far end of the property was a little grove of bare-branched fruit trees, probably apricot and cherry, possibly apple.

Cat would definitely have enough to keep her busy here. And if she was truly busy, how often would she really want to come down and visit her family in Santa Fe?

Rafe did his best to push that thought aside. The important thing was for his sister to be happy, no matter where she ended up. If the prospects for meeting any future life partners out here in Pojoaque were even worse than they'd been in Santa Fe, well, that was Cat's problem to work out. He didn't want to think that she'd given up, but clearly right now she was focused on something other than her love life.

The main house was actually more Tuscan villa in style than pueblo or even Spanish. It stood two stories tall and was faced with stone, topped by a slate roof. It looked sturdy and graceful—an impression that stopped the moment you stepped through the double front doors.

"Well…it'll be a project, that's for sure," Miranda said as she looked around the foyer.

Clearly, the owners had expended all their money and energy on their vines and not too much on their residence. The old oak floor was scratched and stained, and Rafe spied stains on the plaster walls as well, probably from a leaky roof.

Cat shrugged. "I'm okay with that. I have first dibs on staying indefinitely at the Airbnb where I am right now, so if it takes months to get this place ship-shape, that's fine. The important thing is to do it right—this home has good bones, so it'll be worth the effort."

"Maybe we should look at the rest of the house before we make that determination," Rafe suggested. Not that he wanted to shoot down his sister's dreams of creating an idyllic oasis out here in the Pojoaque countryside, but....

His comment made Cat shoot him an annoyed glance, although she didn't argue. "Yes, of course we'll need to go through the whole place. I saw pictures online, but they don't tell all of the story, especially since those pictures were taken when the owners still had their furniture here."

"Lead on," Miranda said. Her big green eyes sparkled with interest, and Rafe guessed that she was already on Cat's side as far as the property was concerned.

They left the foyer and went into the room to their left, which was obviously the dining room. It was long and somewhat narrow, but had a tall, arched window that provided a perfect view of the vineyards. Once the vines had leafed out again, it would probably be spectacular in here.

The kitchen was less promising, but Cat didn't seem put off by the ancient appliances—probably older than she was—or the scratched-up stainless sink. "I'll redo all of this," she said with a wave of her hand. "But at least it's a nice size, and the pantry is huge."

Which it was, with enough space to store supplies for the most enthusiastic of cooks. The rest of the house was much the same way—a lot of cosmetic repair that needed to be done, but Cat's assessment that the bones of the house were good proved to be accurate enough. Rafe didn't even bother to run a rough estimate in his head of what this would all cost, because he knew that such estimates invariably got tossed to the side once you were actually embroiled in a project. However, since Cat could afford it, he didn't bother to make any comments on sort of budget this kind of update would require.

Especially not since she and Miranda were already sharing opinions and ideas, discussing options for flooring and window coverings and everything else. Rafe was content to let them talk, mostly because they both seemed so excited about renovating this house into a showplace, and also because he loved to watch Miranda when she was like this, eyes glowing, cheeks pink with excitement.

Or maybe it was just that he liked to watch Miranda, period. He still had a hard time realizing that someone so strong, so brave, so beautiful, was actually his wife. Maybe it would sink in after they had their "real" wedding ceremony at Loretto

Chapel. He knew her dress-shopping expedition with Cat the day before had been successful, because Miranda had come into the house with a garment bag draped over one arm and a satisfied expression on her face. She'd hidden the dress away in a closet in one of the unused bedrooms and threatened him with all sorts of hexes if he even attempted to take a peek.

"I mean it," she'd said. "It's bad luck to see the wedding gown or the bride before the ceremony, and as far as I'm concerned, we've already had enough bad luck to last us for years."

Rafe had to agree with her on that point. Anyway, he really didn't care about the wedding dress one way or another, as long as Miranda was happy with her choice.

"So I assume you're going to buy it," he said to his sister after they'd finished going over the entire house and had once again gathered in the foyer.

"How could I not buy this place?" Cat replied, a smile touching her lips as she went over and laid a hand on one stained plaster wall. "It needs someone to love it. By the time I'm done, it's going to be spectacular."

"No ghosts?" he teased, but she shook her head, expression suddenly serious.

"No, I don't sense anyone here." She paused for a moment, eyes half shut, as though reaching out to feel the energy of the place. "It looks older than it is, really. The owners say it was built in the late 1960s, and although that's plenty of time for someone to have lived here and died and had their spirit remain behind, I don't feel anything like that. This is a happy place. It has good energy."

Rafe supposed he'd have to take Cat's word for it. She'd always been a lot farther along the "woo-woo" scale than he was, probably because of her witchy talent for communicating with ghosts. Although his own gift of transforming into various wild animals was a rare and valuable one, it also had given him a somewhat pragmatic way of looking at the world. Wolves and coyotes and mountain lions didn't generally have much nonsense about them.

"What about you, Miranda?" he asked then. "Do you feel anything?" After all, her talents were legion, and strong as hell, too. Between the immense powers she'd been born with and the *prima* energy she'd been given, thanks to Louisa's sacrifice, there was a very real possibility that Miranda might be able to sense presences and entities that even Cat couldn't.

"No," Miranda said after a slight pause. "It's just like Cat said—the energy here is good. It feels like…a sanctuary. A place to escape from the world."

After what all of them had suffered at Simon Escobar's hands, Rafe thought they could do with a little sanctuary. At the same time, he hoped Cat wouldn't retreat into this vineyard and not want to come out. She still needed to be part of the Castillo clan, part of their lives.

"Well, it sounds like it's all settled, then," Rafe said.

Cat nodded, dark eyes shining. "Yes, I'll let the owners know I want to take it, and then I just need to shuffle some money around."

A lot of money, Rafe thought, but he didn't say anything. Cat's finances were her own business. Anyway, she'd never been the type to throw cash around. While she wasn't quite as careless about her wardrobe as he tended to be, she also didn't flaunt her Castillo wealth, didn't drop thousands at the pricey boutiques that clustered around Santa Fe's plaza. Really, she hadn't had a lot of things to spend money on all that time she was living at home, so it had been piling up for years.

"Well, let's get the ball rolling," Rafe said, since he knew this was a done deal, and he'd have to step back and let his sister have the freedom to achieve her dream. "It looks like you've just bought yourself a hell of a Christmas present, Cat."

3

Miranda

THAT NIGHT, RAFE AND I HAD CAT AND Eduardo over for dinner, since she had to break the news to him about the winery purchase, and she figured it would be safer to do it with an audience present. Why she was so worried about her father's reaction, I wasn't sure, because Eduardo had always seemed to me to be one of the gentlest men I'd ever met. However, I supposed Cat might be worried that he would see this as an abandonment coming so soon after the death of his wife, although realistically, the vineyard house couldn't possibly be ready for her to move in until the late spring or even early summer. After dealing with the lackadaisical attitude of a lot of the contractors in Santa Fe for just a few minor repairs around the house, I imagined that Cat would have her hands full overseeing such a large project.

Then again, that could be exactly what she wanted.

I had set places for the four of us on the long table in the dining room, and a centerpiece of fresh pine boughs and red velvet bows added a cheery touch. You couldn't see it from the dining room, but a large Noble fir decorated with white lights and a bunch of ornaments I'd found in boxes in the garage held court in the living room, and more pine boughs and red bows had been draped over the mantel. I hadn't been able to do much to the house yet, but filmy draperies at the windows to replace the heavy damask ones that had hung there previously, along with as many Christmas-y touches as I could add without things looking too busy, had done a lot to lighten the mood in the Castillo home. Even Rafe, who in general didn't pay much attention to interior decorating, had complimented me on the way his childhood home looked.

I hoped that the cheerier environment might put Eduardo in a good mood. Certainly when he arrived, a bottle of wine in his hand as an offering, he praised the holiday decor while he looked around, smiling. It had to be difficult to come here when he'd shared this house with Genoveva for so many years, but I didn't see any sorrow or worry in his handsome, refined features, only happiness at a chance to spend the evening with his family.

The three of us went into the dining room, and I sneaked a quick glance at my watch. A little after seven, which meant Cat was running late. Well, she'd had a lot to do this afternoon—I knew she was meeting with the owners of the vineyard, and had brought along a Castillo cousin who was a real estate agent to go over the paperwork and make sure there weren't any red flags. Even so, I was fairly certain that if she'd hit any snags, she would have contacted Rafe or me. However, since neither of us had heard anything, we'd both assumed that everything had gone smoothly. But the smoothest real estate transaction could still be pretty protracted, just because of all the documentation involved.

Luckily, the doorbell rang just a few minutes after Rafe and Eduardo had sat down at the dining table. I excused myself and hurried to answer it. Standing outside was Cat, positively glowing with excitement, her cheeks pink above the wine-colored suede coat she wore.

"I'm sorry I'm late," she said as she unbuttoned her coat, then unwound the scarf she was wearing. Some cold night air had come into the foyer as she entered, and I could tell that the coat and scarf weren't overkill, not at all. I wondered how cold it would really get here; we weren't anywhere near the heart of winter yet, and although I knew something about cold, thanks to living in Flagstaff for part of the year, my family had tended to spend the cold months down in Jerome rather than up in Flag.

"It's fine," I told her. "The lasagna needed to stay in the oven for a bit longer anyway."

"Oh, good." She hung her coat up on the rack that stood in one corner of the foyer. "It took longer to go through all the paperwork than I'd thought, but we finally did plow through it. Luna Rio is now officially mine."

"That's great news," I said, returning her smile. "Your dad's already here, so you can tell him all about it."

Her smile faded a bit. "He's going to think I was way too impulsive about this."

"You don't know that. After all, you took Rafe and me with you to look at the property. It's not as if you blindsided all of us with this."

"I guess so."

She still didn't look convinced, and I didn't bother to argue with her. Yes, she'd taken a big step—and taken on a big responsibility—but she was an adult and could make her own decisions.

In the meantime, though, I needed to get the lasagna out of the oven, and the garlic bread as well. As soon as I mentioned that I needed to check on the food in the kitchen, Cat said, "Let me help you."

"There's not much—just a pan of lasagna, a bowl of salad, and some garlic bread."

"It's enough, though. And it would be rude for me to sit on my butt while you did all the work. I'm surprised Rafe isn't helping you."

"He actually made the garlic bread," I protested. Which he had...under close supervision. Still, he'd helped with spreading the split loaf with melted butter and garlic, and sprinkling the freshly grated Parmesan cheese on top. That had allowed me to put the salad together while he worked. Even when making a relatively simple meal like this one, it was a lot easier to have an extra pair of hands.

"I'd have paid to see that," Cat said as she followed me down the hall and into the kitchen. "Rafe isn't exactly what you'd call domestic."

There was an understatement. However, since we were still in what I could safely call the "honeymoon period," he was usually eager enough to help out when he could.

Really, all I had to do was pull the lasagna out of the oven while Cat retrieved the garlic bread from the toaster oven. She got out a basket and put the bread in it—without having to ask where the basket had been stored, since I hadn't moved much around and so everything was basically put away where it had always been. With her free hand, she picked up the bowl that held the salad. Thus laden, she made her way into the dining room, with me a few feet behind her.

"I see Miranda put you to work right away," Rafe remarked as he took the bowl of salad from her.

"She offered," I said archly, putting the pan of lasagna down on the hot pads I'd already set out to protect the table.

"Yes, I did." Cat lifted an eyebrow at her brother before turning to her father. "Hi, Dad. I hope I didn't make anyone wait too long for dinner."

"No, not long at all," Eduardo said with a smile. "I've only been here five minutes or so."

"Good." She put the basket of garlic bread near her father's place setting and then sat down. Tone a little too falsely cheery, she added, "This all looks great, Miranda. I hope you didn't go to too much work."

"Not much work at all," I replied. Now that all the food had been brought out, I figured it was safe to sit down in my normal spot, to Rafe's right. When we'd eaten our first meal at this table, he'd tried to get me to sit at the head, since that place should be reserved for the *prima*, but I'd demurred. It felt strange for me to take that spot, no matter what the Castillo tradition might have been. The table was far too long to think about putting Eduardo at the other end, so he was seated to Rafe's left, with Cat next to him. A little lopsided, but at least we wouldn't need megaphones to communicate with one another.

"Rafe tells me that you're an excellent cook, Miranda," Eduardo said as he took a piece of garlic bread from the basket and passed it along to his daughter.

"I had a good teacher," I said, trying to fight the flush of embarrassment that rose in my cheeks. Maybe one of these days I'd get better at accepting compliments. "My Great-Aunt Rachel. She's amazing."

"And so are you," Rafe said. "Even though you're going red as a tomato right now."

I did my best to pretend I didn't know what he was talking about. "Anyway, I like to cook. I can't wait until Christmas—I've always wanted to try making a goose."

"You need to be careful, though," Cat remarked as she dished herself some salad. "Rosa tried to roast a goose for Christmas dinner one year and almost caught her oven on fire."

"Goose is very fatty," Eduardo observed, a certain amused light dancing in his dark eyes. I had the impression that he might have gotten a certain perverse pleasure in seeing his bossy older sister prove she wasn't infallible. Not that he would probably admit it if pressed, but it was nice to see that Eduardo wasn't quite as angelic as I'd thought.

"I'll be careful," I said.

"You're sure you want to cook Christmas dinner so close to the wedding?" Rafe asked. I knew he wasn't revealing any deep, dark secrets, since we'd already let Eduardo know the ceremony had been scheduled for the twenty-third, and he in turn had gotten the word out to the Castillo clan. "I thought you might want to get away for a few days."

I shook my head. "No, I'd rather stay here. We can plan a vacation for later on if we want, but I want to spend Christmas in our new home." Well, my new home anyway. This house was certainly not new to Rafe, but maybe he looked on it with fresh eyes now that he was living here with his wife, rather than under his mother's thumb.

"That actually sounds great," he said. "A nice Santa Fe Christmas."

"We'll all have to do the Canyon Road walk," Cat suggested.

Puzzled, I tilted my head at her. "What's that?"

"Something we've been doing here in Santa Fe since before I was born," Eduardo said. "Canyon Road is closed to vehicle traffic, and the galleries and shops stay open and offer snacks and desserts and hot cider and coffee."

"There are bonfires, too," Cat put in. "And most of the buildings have Christmas lights or farolinos—"

"What's a farolino?" I asked. I knew I'd never heard that word before.

"Luminarias," Rafe said. "You know, the little paper bags with candles inside them?"

Right. We'd decorated with luminarias at the Jerome house, having them march up the front walk to the big porch. As a child, I'd been fascinated by them, by the warm glow of the candles inside the brown paper bags. Canyon Road was picturesque enough on its own, with its old adobe buildings and tall trees. I could only imagine how spectacular it must be with the walls and rooflines of the structures there picked out by glowing farolinos.

"And there are carolers, and sometimes it feels as if everyone in Santa Fe is there," Cat said. "I can't imagine spending Christmas Eve any other way."

It did sound like a lot of fun. The house was so close, we'd be able to walk over without having to worry about finding parking on one of the streets adjacent to Canyon Road. "Okay, the Canyon Road walk on Christmas Eve, and then both of you over for dinner on Christmas Day."

"And your parents, too?" Rafe asked. "After all, they'll already be here for the wedding."

"I'll have to check," I replied. From the way my mother had talked, it sounded as if she and my father just wanted to come to Santa Fe to see me safely married, and then they'd pop right back to Jerome to spend Christmas there. And by "pop," they meant teleporting, rather than spending hours on the road. Whether they'd want to stay, I didn't know for sure. The past few Christmases, everyone had gone up to their house for dinner—Ian and Emily and their spouses, and the grandchildren. The kids grew up so fast when they were little like that. Would my parents want to miss spending the holiday with them?

I honestly couldn't say for sure. To my relief, no one pressed me on the subject. We still had a couple of weeks to get it all figured out anyway.

Rafe lifted an eyebrow at Cat and inclined his head toward Eduardo, who was concentrating on scooping up a forkful of lasagna and therefore distracted. She swallowed and looked suddenly apprehensive. *Go on,* he mouthed at her.

"Um, Dad," she began, and Eduardo looked up from his food.

"What is it, Cat?"

She fidgeted with the napkin in her lap, then said, "I found a house. It's in Pojoaque. Miranda and Rafe went with me to look at it yesterday, and today I bought it."

For a moment, Eduardo just stared at her, almost as if he hadn't heard her correctly. "A house?" he repeated.

"Yes. Actually, it's the Luna Rio winery. Remember how Seth was talking about it at the restaurant the other day? It sounded like just the kind of place I was looking for, and it turned out that it was. I didn't want to take the risk of someone else snapping it up, so I went ahead and bought the place."

"You don't know anything about making wine," Eduardo said, echoing the same argument I'd made only a few days earlier. His expression was calm enough, but I could see the furrow between his brows as he frowned faintly.

"I'm not going to make wine," Cat replied. I couldn't see her hands, but I had a feeling that she was continuing to play with the napkin in her lap. "I'll keep the vines and keep producing grapes because they're valuable, but I'm just going to sell the crop to other local wineries. They're always looking for New Mexico grapes because none of the winemakers around here want to admit to using grapes from California and Arizona."

"It seems you've thought about this a great deal," Eduardo said, still in that same mild tone.

"Well, I didn't want you to think I was going

off half-cocked about this whole thing." She paused there and appeared to study her father's expression. Words stumbling a bit, she went on, "I —I didn't want you to get angry with me for doing something impulsive."

"Angry?" He smiled and shook his head. "Why on earth would I be angry with you? Your money is your own to do with as you please, and you've made it clear enough that your situation here in town was only a temporary one until you found a place that suited you. I might wish it was a little closer, but Pojoaque isn't so far away."

"Thanks, Dad," Cat said, her eyes a little too bright. She blinked before continuing. "And I won't be moving for a while, anyway. I can't really get anyone in to give me estimates on the work that needs to be done until after the first of the year, and then I have a feeling it's going to be a few more months before the place is ready."

"That long?" For the first time, Eduardo looked truly concerned. "I hope you haven't bought a money pit, Cat."

"Oh, it'll probably feel like one by the time I'm done," she said cheerfully, obviously not at all daunted by the work that lay ahead of her. "But in the end, it'll be worth the effort."

"It really is a beautiful place," I said. While I was relieved that Cat's father didn't seem too dismayed by the massive purchase she'd just made,

I also wanted him to know that Rafe and I were fully on board with the idea as well. "The house definitely needs some updating, but as far as we were able to tell, it's mostly cosmetic work that needs to be done."

"But you don't know for sure?" Eduardo asked. "Cat, didn't you have a building inspection done before you signed the paperwork?"

"No," she responded, then went on quickly, "Don't worry, though—Alyssa had them add a clause in the contract that the purchase could be reversed if any major structural issues were found."

An expression of relief passed over his face. "Well, that's good. I'm glad you took your cousin with you to help with the contract—and I'm glad that Rafe and Miranda also approve of the house."

"It's a really impressive piece of property," Rafe said. He'd been mostly quiet up until then, eating lasagna and salad and garlic bread, interspersed with sips of chianti, but it seemed as though he thought he should chime in now as well. "I don't doubt that in a few years, Cat will make back her investment. New Mexico grapes are at a premium right now, so she should be able to get top dollar for her harvests."

He hadn't said anything to me, but I had a feeling that Rafe had been doing some quiet research on the side, trying to ascertain just how much money the Luna Rio grapes were worth. Apparently, what he'd found had reassured him. It wasn't that Cat couldn't afford to pay for the old vineyard and never get anything out of it, but if she could be self-sustaining, all the better.

"That sounds very promising," Eduardo said. Judging by the way he relaxed back into his chair, I thought Rafe's words had been more than welcome. Directing his next words to Rafe and me, he went on, "Now, I suppose we should discuss your reception. We'll have it at the restaurant, just as we'd planned the first time, but is there anything about it that you'd like to change?"

Considering that I'd never made it to the first reception, had fled to the false refuge of Simon's "apartment," I didn't feel I was qualified to comment on anything that might need to be altered. Really, all I wanted was the sort of pleasant, low-key gathering where everyone could enjoy themselves without having to expend too much effort.

Surprisingly, Cat came to my rescue, saying, "I thought everything looked beautiful, but maybe you could give the reception space more of a holiday feel somehow."

I hadn't really asked Rafe what he'd done after I'd teleported out of Loretto Chapel, leaving him standing at the altar by himself. Those memories had been painful enough that I had no desire to revisit them, and I knew he felt the same way, wanted to focus on what lay ahead of us, not behind. As far as I could tell, though, it sounded as if he'd avoided the reception, and so Cat would have been the one who'd actually seen how the hall was decorated, or what kind of food had been served.

"That sounds like a good idea," I said. "Maybe sort of a 'winter wonderland' feel—white fairy lights and crystal ornaments, everything white and silver." Which would also echo the beaded and jeweled ornaments on my new wedding gown, although I kept that particular detail to myself. I didn't want to give Rafe even a hint of what the dress looked like. Probably I was being paranoid, but after surviving Simon Escobar's evil plots, I thought it was better not to take any chances.

"I think that would be beautiful," Eduardo said. "If you have time, possibly you and Rafe and Cat can choose what you'd like to use for decorations."

Rafe didn't look terribly enthusiastic about this suggestion, although I figured he would gamely go along if pressed. Cat, on the other hand, seemed ready to go.

"Oh, that'll be fun. There's this great party rental place down in Albuquerque we can go to. Just let me know when."

"My schedule is pretty open for now," I

replied. "Why don't you make sure you have the house squared away, and then we'll figure out a good time to go to Albuquerque and see what we can find."

"How about next Monday, just to be safe?" she suggested. "I can't imagine anything with the house taking much longer than that, especially since I can't start any real work for a few more weeks."

"Sounds good." I glanced over at Rafe, who looked almost relieved that he was being left safely out of these negotiations. "You're sure you don't want to come along?"

"Positive," he replied, so quickly that both Cat and I couldn't help but share a conspiratorial chuckle.

"Okay," I said. "We won't twist your arm."

From there, the conversation moved on to the food we'd be serving at the reception, and the most delicate way to let people know that we didn't expect them to get us any other presents. One of the spare bedrooms here at the house was still stacked full of gifts from the first wedding. Both Rafe and I knew we needed to get in there and unwrap everything and make a database of who'd given us what and write thank-you notes, but it was a task we'd both been putting off. However, I knew we'd have to take care of it before this second wedding ceremony took place, or it was going to look pretty bad.

At the end of the evening, Eduardo and Cat both said goodbye and headed out together, and I shut the door and looked over at Rafe.

"He took it well," I said.

"I was pretty sure he would." A slight shrug, and he came over and pulled me to him, wrapping his arms around me. "My dad knows how to roll with the punches as they come. And it could be worse—at least she hasn't fallen in love with someone down in Las Cruces or something and is moving four hours away."

"True."

We went into the dining room and began to clear away the plates. Once that task was done, I got the pan with the leftover lasagna—not that there was much left; we'd all done a pretty good job of demolishing it—and put some foil over the top before I set the pan in the refrigerator. In the meantime, Rafe got to work rinsing off the knives and forks and dishes so he could place them in the dishwasher.

"I like this," I said, and he lifted an eyebrow at me.

"Doing dishes?"

"No," I replied. "Just…this. Being domestic together. Having a quiet evening with family. It's almost like—"

"Almost like none of that stuff with Simon happened?" Rafe finished for me.

"Something like that. I mean, obviously it did, or I wouldn't be *prima* of the Castillo clan now, but it's just good to have the feeling that things are settling down."

"I hope so," he said as he shut the dishwasher door. "I think I've had enough excitement to last me a lifetime."

Now it was my turn to lift an eyebrow at him. "You sure about that? Because I was thinking that I had a few ideas about how we might end this evening."

He went and wiped his damp hands on the towel that hung from the magnet on the side of the refrigerator, then came over to me and took me in his arms. After a hearty kiss that tasted of chianti and garlic bread, he murmured in my ear, "Oh, I'll never get tired of *that* kind of excitement."

Then he scooped me up in his arms. I gave an excited laugh, and clung to him as he took me up the stairs. As he laid me down on the bed and gave me another very thorough kiss, I thought I could get used to married life. It was worth everything we'd been through to end up where we were now.

I only hoped things would always stay this way.

4

Rafe

ONLY TEN MINUTES OR SO AFTER MIRANDA and Cat had headed out for their expedition to Albuquerque, Rafe's phone rang. He pulled it out of his pocket, wondering if maybe they'd forgotten something or—God forbid—had experienced some kind of car trouble.

The number displayed on the screen wasn't Miranda's, though. It was his cousin Sophia, Tony's mother. Looking down at the screen on his cell phone, Rafe couldn't quite keep himself from frowning. He had no idea why Sophia would be calling him, although he doubted it had anything to do with the upcoming wedding. Tony had once again been pressed into best-man duty, although he'd joked that if this wedding backfired, too, he was washing his hands of the whole business. At any rate, Tony's mother had been invited to the ceremony, of course, but that was the extent of her involvement.

"Hi, Sophia," Rafe said after swiping on his phone's screen to accept the call. "What's up?"

Her voice sounding somewhat strange, his cousin asked, "Rafe, would you mind coming over? This isn't the sort of thing I want to discuss on the phone."

The request immediately made his spider sense start tingling. "You afraid the NSA is listening in or something?"

Although Sophia wasn't nearly as devil-may-care as her son, usually she had a pretty good sense of humor about things. Now, though, she only said, "No, nothing like that. It's just that I've been going through the items taken from the house where Simon Escobar was staying, and…." She trailed off there, something that sounded like a sigh coming through the cell phone's tiny speaker. "It's something I'd like to talk to you about."

"Why me and not Miranda?" He didn't exactly like where this conversation was going, but he figured that it was really Miranda's responsibility as *prima* to handle this sort of thing, as much as she'd tried to avoid anything to do with Simon Escobar once he was safely out of the way.

A long pause. When she finally spoke, Sophia

sounded obviously diffident. "Because Miranda's still finding her way as *prima,* and I'd rather talk to you. Once you've heard what I have to say, you can approach her with the information if you want. All right?"

"All right," Rafe echoed. He didn't like the sound of any of this, but better to go hear what his cousin had discovered. "I can be over in about ten minutes. Is that okay?"

"That's great," she responded, relief clear in her tone. "I'm looking forward to it."

He didn't know if he was, but he'd already committed to going over to Sophia's house. Might as well get this over with.

After checking his phone to make sure he hadn't missed any calls or texts from Miranda—which of course he hadn't—Rafe went to the garage and got into his Jeep, then headed up to the Hyde Park area in the foothills above Santa Fe where Sophia's home was located. A long time ago, before his mother had become *prima,* Rafe had lived here as well. He still experienced a small pang as he passed the turn-off that led to one of his favorite hiking trails, a twinge at the way his life had changed forever when his grandmother Isabel died and Genoveva had to take over as *prima.*

Well, all that was ancient history. Now, through a twist of fate—and the intervention of

his sister Louisa, who should've been *prima*—
Miranda was the head witch of the Castillos, and
he was her consort. But Miranda had already
shown that she was going to be a very different
sort of *prima* from Genoveva. Just the feeling he
experienced whenever he walked into his house
was enough to tell him that. It already felt lighter
and happier, as though Miranda's very spirit had
somehow infused the walls of the old
adobe home.

He turned off onto the street that led into
Sophia's neighborhood, winding up and away
from Hyde Park Road and into the hills. Her
community was gated, but those sorts of security
measures weren't enough to keep out any witches
or warlocks; Rafe merely waved a hand at the little
box that controlled the gate and then drove his
Wrangler through as though he had every right to
be there.

Sophia's big Spanish-style house was located at
the end of a cul-de-sac, on a piece of land that
topped a promontory and afforded a spectacular
set of views west across Santa Fe and all the way to
the Jemez Mountains and Los Alamos. Rafe
pulled up into the driveway and parked, then got
out and headed toward the front door. They'd had
some early snow a few days back, and it still
gleamed pale and cold from some of the more
sheltered spots in the front yard.

Almost as soon as he'd rung the doorbell, his cousin Sophia was at the front door. She was in her middle fifties, slim, but in the sort of taut, strained way that seemed to indicate she watched every bite that went into her mouth and was vigilant about never missing a Pilates class.

"Come on in, Rafe," she said, stepping aside so he could enter the foyer. He'd only been here a few times, but the house was as pale and elegant as he remembered, cool travertine on the floors, the walls the world's lightest shade of parchment. "Why don't we go into the living room?"

"Sure," he replied, and followed her to that room, which was also pale, with its bone leather couches and iron coffee table topped by inlaid stone in shades of cream and beige. A pitcher of water sat on top of that table, accompanied by a pair of glasses.

"Some water?" Sophia asked, and he nodded.

She poured a glass for each of them, then handed one to Rafe. He sat down, acutely aware of the expensive leather of the couch crinkling beneath him. The place looked like a model home, but in its own way, it was just as off-putting as his own house had been before Miranda started putting in her own little touches to make it more homey. More than once, Rafe had wondered how Tony had turned out so free-wheeling when his mother was so uptight, but he figured that Tony's devil-may-care attitude had to be a direct reaction to Sophia's rigid self-control.

Besides, her talent wasn't an easy one to live with. She had the ability to read any type of magical spell or book, no matter what language it might have been written in. Since many magical writings tended to explore the darker side of the powers that witches and warlocks possessed, Rafe guessed it couldn't be easy to be exposed to that sort of thing.

No one else in the clan had anything like Sophia's magical power, and so it fell to her to be the guardian of any magical items that were remotely questionable…which was also why she'd become the keeper of Simon Escobar's personal effects, so to speak.

Rafe took a sip from the glass of water she'd handed him, then asked, "What's this about, Sophia? Did you find something in those spell books Escobar left behind?"

Her normally full mouth thinned. "It's not really what's *in* them…more the very fact of their existence."

"Well, I didn't think he'd be carrying around anything as simple as a couple of paperback mysteries," Rafe said.

"I wish it were that easy." Sophia lifted her own glass and drank as well. "Frankly, I'm having a hard time figuring out what the de la Paz clan was doing with those sorts of books in the first place. They're extremely dangerous."

"What's in them, anyway?" Rafe didn't know whether he should even have asked that question, but his curiosity had gotten the better of him. "I mean, obviously there were spells about calling demons, or Escobar wouldn't have used them to summon his own private demon army." And the Lord of Chaos, the otherworldly entity Simon had called to do his bidding, although Rafe figured it was better not to mention the demon lord's existence, the way he seemed to now be trapped in this world with no way to get back to his own plane. Everyone who'd been present for the final showdown with Simon Escobar—including Sophia's son Tony—had been sworn to secrecy about the presence of the powerful demon, especially since it turned out that he was more or less sympathetic to the Castillos' cause. Besides, since the Lord of Chaos had made himself scarce ever since he helped them defeat Escobar, there didn't seem to be much point in bringing up the subject now.

"Demon summoning is only a very small part of it," Sophia said. Her face was pale, but she seemed composed enough, possibly relieved now that she had someone to talk to. "Blood magic, animal and human sacrifice, terrible spells to bend others to the magic-user's will…I could go on, but I think you can get the picture."

"Yes," Rafe replied, more than a little shaken. There were reasons why that sort of magic had been forbidden hundreds of years earlier. It was terrible and immoral…which was probably exactly why Simon Escobar had sought it out. Rafe supposed he should be glad that the dark warlock had been focused on demon summoning and not some of the even blacker spells that existed within the grimoires he'd stolen. What if he'd used one of those mind-control spells on Miranda? Would her innate magical powers have been enough to save her?

He really didn't want to think about that. In a way, it was good that Simon had harbored such a twisted affection for Miranda—he'd wanted her to love him for himself, and not because of any spell he'd cast on her. Otherwise, he might have tried to bend her to his will, might have….

Enough of that. Rafe blinked, and saw that Sophia was watching him with concern in her hazel eyes. He cleared his throat and asked, "Why not send the books back to the de la Paz clan? They belong to them."

She gave a regretful shake of her head. "That was my first thought, but then I realized it wasn't a good solution at all. Rafe, I'm not sure the de la Pazes even know the books are missing. Otherwise, surely they would have reached out to us, since Miranda's parents know what happened with Simon Escobar and must have shared that information with the other Arizona witch clans. If they're that careless with items that are so clearly dangerous, how can I in good conscience send the books back to them?"

Rafe had to admit, she had a point. On the other hand, if the de la Pazes knew that Simon had plundered their various caches of magical writings, maybe they kept quiet because they were doing an inventory of their spell books and didn't want to say anything to the Castillos until they knew for sure what was missing.

Or maybe they were plain old embarrassed. Rafe knew he would be, if he had to confess to the other witch clans in the area that a dark warlock had been able to waltz right in and walk away with some of the rare and dangerous items his family had supposedly been keeping safe for generations.

"I see your point," he allowed. "It could be that they're still trying to figure out what Simon took. I don't know all that much about it, but, as far as I've been able to tell from a few things Miranda has said, it's not as though the de la Pazes keep everything in one central location. Their *prima* has her own library of grimoires, and there are others in the clan who have collections of spell books as well."

Sophia's lips pursed. "If they're going to be so haphazard, then again, do you really feel it's a good idea to send the books back to them?"

"Do you *want* to keep them?" Rafe asked, genuinely curious. If Sophia thought they were such a burden, why wouldn't she be doing whatever she could to get the books back to their rightful owners, despite her misgivings?

"Of course not," she replied at once. "But neither do I want them to go someplace where they might not be treated with the respect they deserve."

A wry smile tugging at his mouth, he said, "I have a feeling the de la Pazes have probably learned their lesson on this one."

For a moment, Sophia didn't reply. Her expertly plucked brows pulled together as she frowned slightly. At least a pucker formed in the middle of her forehead, which meant that she hadn't yet gone so far as to get filler injections to slow down any telltale signs of aging. "Maybe," she said with some reluctance. "But even if they try to be more careful, will it be enough? Thank God that dark warlocks are few and far between, but it doesn't mean they don't exist. It's possible that word has gotten out in certain circles about the de la Paz clan's various caches of spell books. If that's the case, then there could still be a danger." Her fingers, manicured but bare of polish, knotted together.

Rafe hadn't even thought about that particular possibility. From what he'd been able to tell, Simon Escobar had been a lone wolf, acting purely on his own without help from anyone else. Not that he'd needed the help—he was the most powerful warlock Rafe had ever seen. Even Miranda, with all her spectacular abilities and the assist from her newly acquired *prima* powers, had barely been able to defeat him. However, there was still the question of his father Joaquin. He'd come from somewhere in Central America—"Escobar" was a fairly common name in El Salvador —but no one had been able to find out very much about precisely where in El Salvador he'd come from, or what he'd done before he came to the U.S. For all anyone knew, there could be a veritable hotbed of dark warlocks and witches down in that part of the world, although that was a prospect Rafe really didn't want to contemplate.

"But they probably wouldn't know we have some of the books they're looking for—if anyone really is looking for them other than the de la Pazes," Rafe said. "Simon didn't tell Miranda everything, of course, but it sounded as though he took the grimoires and didn't stick around to see what happened next, which means there's not much chance that anyone else had any idea what he'd done."

"I hope you're right." Sophia tapped her fingers on the knee of her dark jeans, the diamond anniversary band on her left hand glinting in the pale afternoon sunlight that came through the living room's windows. Her husband, another Castillo cousin, was a lawyer, and probably at work in his offices not too far from the state's capital building, affectionately known as the Roundhouse. The two of them projected an image of a perfect upper-middle-class couple, and Rafe was fairly certain that none of their neighbors in this pricey development had any idea that they happened to be living next door to a family of witches and warlocks.

And he kind of doubted any of those neighbors would be too thrilled to find out that Sophia was hiding a stash of stolen grimoires somewhere in her house. That sort of thing could definitely bring down property values.

"I just wanted you to know what we're dealing with here," she went on. "There really isn't an ideal solution, but it's probably best if I hold on to the books for now. If the de la Pazes come to us directly—and if they have an accurate list of what was taken from them—then I suppose we'll have to return the books. In the meantime, I'll do what I can to make sure they're safe."

What that would be, Rafe didn't know for sure. Yes, Sophia's magic allowed her to read what was in those books of dark spells, but that was about it. Her husband's talent for being able to tell when people were lying stood him in good stead in his day job as an attorney, but it wouldn't do much when it came to protecting the dangerous, valuable grimoires that had come into their possession.

"Let me talk to Miranda about that," Rafe said. "I think at the very least she'll want to come over and cast a protection spell on the books or something. Those spells worked pretty well keeping everyone safe when Escobar was trying to attack the clan, so I have to think they'll do as well when protecting inanimate objects."

"That's a good idea," Sophia responded, looking relieved. "Her magic is very strong."

Yes, it was, and thank God for that, or Rafe was pretty sure he wouldn't be sitting here now and having this conversation with his cousin. He'd probably be dead, and Miranda.... He drew in a breath and said, "She's in Albuquerque today, doing some shopping with Cat for the reception, but I'll talk to her as soon as she gets home."

A smile, and Sophia said, "Thank you, Rafe. I appreciate that, especially with all the planning I know you need to do for the wedding."

"Not a problem." He reflected that there

wasn't as much planning as some might think—the invitations had already been handled, the venue chosen, Miranda's wedding dress purchased. They still needed to handle the flowers and the cake, but really, they could probably just order the same things they'd had for the first ceremony and call it a day. However, since he didn't want his cousin to think he was being nonchalant about all the work involved, he added, "Cat and Dad are helping, too, so I think between the four of us, we've got everything handled."

"I'm glad to hear it. Everyone is really looking forward to seeing you two married."

Which of course he and Miranda already were, but Rafe thought he knew what Sophia meant. In a way, he needed the reality of the ceremony as well, so it could tell him that they truly were husband and wife.

"We're looking forward to it, too," he said, then got up from the couch where he'd been sitting. "I should probably go—I need to be home when Miranda and Cat get back from Albuquerque, just in case there's stuff they need brought in from the car."

"Of course." Sophia stood as well. "Let me walk you to the door."

She saw him out, and he waved and said goodbye before heading down the front walk to where his Jeep was parked in the driveway. He reflected that it was a good thing he'd had it inspected mechanically from top to bottom after the bodywork was done—Simon Escobar had really smashed the hell out of the poor thing when he tipped the Wrangler on its side during their final confrontation—because at least now Rafe knew there wasn't any chance of the vehicle dripping oil on the pristine concrete of Sophia's driveway, which was just as immaculate as the rest of her house.

As he drove away, though, the smile he'd put on as he'd said goodbye to his cousin faded away. During the past few weeks, he and Miranda had done basically whatever they could to avoid the topic of Simon Escobar. He was done, in the past, and they had better things to focus on. Now, though, it was as if his ghost had returned to haunt them, thanks to those damn books he'd left behind at his house in La Cienega.

Unfortunately, they'd have to deal with that ghost…and hope they could finally lay it to rest.

5

Miranda

RAFE WAS SITTING AT THE KITCHEN TABLE when I returned from Albuquerque. Cat and I had had a great time picking out decorations for the reception hall, and had placed a much larger order with the party rental company than I'd first imagined. Then again, this was a big deal, a way to make our legitimate to all the Castillos. I needed to ensure that everything went as smoothly as possible, and that meant throwing a wedding reception that didn't look like some hastily slapped-together affair.

Because I hadn't really bought anything, had only placed an order for lights and decorations, I didn't walk into the house with anything except my purse slung over my shoulder. Cat had dropped me off and sped away after apologizing for not coming in. While we were at the party rental place, she'd gotten a text from one of the contractors she'd been negotiating with. He'd had a cancellation and was available to take a look at the Pojoaque property, and so she didn't have any time to spare, but needed to get back on the road as soon as possible.

I didn't mind that she needed to get going. While I didn't want to bore Rafe too much with elaborate descriptions of what I had planned for the reception, I figured it couldn't hurt to give him just a little sneak peek. However, judging by the abstracted frown he wore as I approached the kitchen table, I had a feeling he wouldn't be too interested in descriptions of white and silver topiaries or bare birch branches with twinkle LEDs embedded in them.

"What's the matter?" I asked, slipping my purse over the back of a chair before I pulled it out and sat down. "You look like a storm cloud."

"Sorry," Rafe replied, and reached up to push back the too-long piece of hair that always wanted to fall into the middle of his forehead. "I just had to run over to my cousin Sophia's house. Tony's mother," he added, since apparently he could tell from my expression that I didn't have the faintest idea who Sophia was.

"Oh," I said. "He's not pulling out of the

wedding, is he? I mean, I suppose we could find someone else to be best man, but—"

"Nothing like that," Rafe broke in. "Basically, she's the one who got stuck babysitting the spell books that were taken from the house in La Cienega. She wanted to talk to me about what we should do with them."

Right. Handling the disposal of those grimoires had been one of many items on a long to-do list, a task that I'd mentally filed in the "after the wedding" category and promptly forgot about. "Shouldn't we send them back to the de la Paz clan?"

"That was my first suggestion, but Sophia had several reservations, all of which were valid enough. It's probably better if we sit on them for now."

I could feel a frown of my own pulling at my brows. Hanging on to the grimoires didn't seem like a very good idea to me, but if Rafe had discussed the problem with Sophia and they'd both agreed that the books should stay for now, I wasn't about to argue with them. "Okay," I said. "It sounds as if you have the problem handled."

"Maybe," Rafe allowed. "All the same, we both thought it would be a good idea to have you cast a protection spell on the books and on Sophia's house…just to be safe."

"Sure," I said. Those protection spells had

worked well enough to keep Simon Escobar away from most of the Castillo clan, so I had no reason to believe they wouldn't be equally effective now. It was definitely wise to employ some sort of safeguard, because while I wouldn't have touched any of those books with a ten-foot pole, I knew there were unscrupulous witches and warlocks in the world who would be all too eager to get their hands on even one of them. "Did Sophia say when?"

"No time like the present." His expression lightened a bit, and he said, "I figured I could take you out to dinner after we were done, maybe up at Ten Thousand Waves?"

"What's that?" I was beginning to get more familiar with Santa Fe as time wore on, but there was still so much about it that I knew nothing about.

"It's a resort up in the Hyde Park area. The restaurant there is pretty amazing. I've been meaning to take you anyway, but since Sophia's house is only about five minutes away—"

"This is the perfect opportunity to go," I finished for him. "Sounds like fun. Just give me a few minutes to get freshened up, and then we can head over to your cousin's place."

"I'll call her and let her know we'll be over soon."

I nodded, then went upstairs to change out of

my slouchy sweater and into a jacket with a simple camisole underneath. Since I was already wearing slim jeans and high boots, I figured the ensemble should pass muster in just about anything except Santa Fe's snootiest restaurants. A few passes with a hairbrush, a refresh of my lip gloss, and I figured I was good to go.

Rafe had slipped a leather jacket over his long-sleeved T-shirt, about as far as he was willing to go in the "dressing up" department unless he was attending a wedding or a funeral. Still, he looked so handsome that I had to go over and squeeze his hand. At first I'd meant to give him a quick kiss, but I realized I would only end up getting lip gloss all over him.

"Sophia's waiting for us," he said, pressing my fingers briefly before he let go.

"Okay."

We went out to the garage and got in his Jeep. By this point, I'd been around so many Castillos that meeting another one didn't send the same kind of butterflies to my stomach as this sort of encounter might have only a few weeks earlier. Despite my lack of apprehension, I found myself wondering about this cousin Sophia—whether her son Tony resembled her, whether they were at all alike in terms of personality…what her specific magical talent might be.

Hers hadn't been one of the households given

faulty magical protection by Rafe's sister Malena, and so I'd never been out this way before. I looked around with some interest as we climbed out of Santa Fe's downtown area and up toward the foothills.

"If you keep going on this road, you'll get to the ski resort, but we'll be pulling off before then," Rafe told me.

"Do you ski?" I asked. The topic really hadn't come up before this, although I knew I'd read somewhere that the Sangre de Cristos usually got enough snow to offer some decent skiing.

He shook his head. "No. I snowboarded some when I was in high school. Tony and I used to come up here together when we had the time. But I broke my leg my senior year, and even though Yesenia fixed me right up, my mother wasn't too keen on me doing any more snowboarding after that." A grin, and he added, "Actually, I wasn't that keen, either, or I would have kept it up just to spite her. It's great to have a clan healer and everything, but a broken leg still hurts like hell no matter how you heal up afterward."

That was true enough. Having a healer around to treat your injuries might keep you out of the hospital, but a broken bone was a broken bone. Luckily, I'd never done anything worse to myself than sprain my ankle one time when I was hiking around Mingus Mountain, but even the sprain had hurt badly enough that I was all too happy to skip experiencing anything more severe.

"Still," he went on, "it's pretty up here after a good snowfall, even if all you want to do is sit in the restaurant at the ski resort and watch everyone else as they ski. We'll have to come up sometime this winter."

"That sounds like fun," I said, and it did. Something normal and very un-witch-like, which was about my speed these days. While I was glad to have magic at my disposal should I need it, and proud to carry the Castillo *prima* powers within me, I thought we were all due for a nice, quiet winter.

He nodded, then said, "Sophia's talent is being able to read any sort of magical spell or grimoire. That was why she got possession of the books—it seemed wisest to have someone who actually knew what they were guarding take charge of them."

His tone was matter-of-fact enough, but I couldn't help feeling a bit of a chill move down my spine. Neither the McAllisters nor the Wilcoxes had much to do with grimoires, and the thought of all those spells being written down where anyone could access them made me nervous. I'd be glad when they were safely hidden behind a protection spell.

Rafe turned off onto a road that wound further up into the hills, and paused for a moment to wave his hand at the electronic gate at the entrance to the development. It was the first time I'd seen anything like that in Santa Fe, but I supposed that the residents of the neighborhood wanted to make sure no wayward skiers couldn't find their way in here by accident. This appeared to be a pretty upscale area, each house on a substantial piece of land, some of them so hilly and steep, I wondered how anyone could have thought they were workable homesites.

After a few minutes, Rafe turned again, this time onto a short cul-de-sac that was relatively level compared to the places we'd passed so far. At the end of the cul-de-sac was a large Spanish-style home; he pulled into the driveway there and turned off the engine. "Here we are," he said, somewhat unnecessarily.

I got out of the Jeep and followed him to the front door. Despite my earlier calm, I couldn't help experiencing a few butterflies in my stomach as I waited at the front door. After all, this wasn't purely a social call. Sophia was expecting me to protect her and her family from anyone who might come seeking those terrible books Simon Escobar had left behind, and I had to do my damnedest to ensure I didn't make any mistakes.

The door opened, and a woman probably five or so years older than my mother looked out at us. She was very attractive, with sleek dark hair that fell perfectly onto her slender shoulders and the high cheekbones and elegant nose that so many of the Castillos seemed to share, but there was also something too tense about her, as if she spent a lot of time and effort making sure she presented a perfect face to the world.

"Sophia, this is Miranda," Rafe said. "Miranda, this is my cousin Sophia."

"I'm so glad to meet you," Sophia said, then opened the door a bit wider. "Please, come in. Miranda, I saw you in passing when I was at the house for Marco's funeral reception, but you probably don't remember me."

I shook my head and sent her an apologetic smile. "I'm sorry—that was such a crazy, terrible day that most of it is still a blur to me."

"I understand." She gestured toward a hallway that opened off the foyer. "Let me take you to where I've been keeping the books."

Rafe and I followed her past a living room furnished in muted shades of beige and cream, a dining room done in similar tones, and into what was clearly a family space. A large TV was mounted to one wall, and there were several overstuffed couches upholstered in soft brown linen.

Sophia went past all that to a door set into one wall. Hand on the knob, she turned slightly back toward us and said, "When we bought the house, the previous owners had left a safe in here.

We never really had need of it, but we left it where it was since we didn't have anything else we needed to do with this space. Now I'm glad we never got rid of it."

Looking over her shoulder, I could just make out the dark outlines of a safe about five feet high set up against the back wall of the oversized closet, or whatever it was. Sophia went into the little space and over to the safe, then turned the combination lock set into the door. Clever of them to use the safe; while all witches and warlocks could open standard locks with tumblers—or bypass electronic security like the gate that guarded Sophia's tract of expensive homes—anything with a combination was just as inaccessible to us as it was to an ordinary civilian. Even if a dark witch or warlock somehow figured out what was being hidden here, they'd have a tough time getting past this particular safe.

The safe's door slowly swung open, revealing a collection of some twenty or thirty leather-bound books sitting on the shelves inside the safe. Although from this distance they appeared innocuous enough, I fancied I could feel the evil drifting out from them, like some sort of foul perfume floating on the air.

"Did you take an inventory of them?" I asked.

"Yes," Sophia said. "I wrote it all down—I thought it was probably better not to store that information on my computer." She went up to the safe and lifted a single sheet of lined paper from the safe's top shelf, then came over and handed it to me.

I glanced at the paper briefly, cold trickling down my spine. Some of the titles were Latin, others Spanish, a few of them in a language I didn't even recognize. Only one was in English: *The Lore and Summoning of Demons.*

How Sophia had been able to record all those titles accurately, I wasn't sure...until I realized that her own particular talent had probably guided her, providing her with the knowledge she needed.

"Thanks," I said, and gave her back the note. "You might as well keep the list in the safe, too. It's probably, well, safer."

Despite the grimness of the situation, Rafe smiled slightly. "That sounds like a good idea."

Sophia nodded and replaced the piece of paper on the shelf, then closed the door of the safe and spun the combination lock a few times before giving me an expectant look. "How do you want to handle this?" she asked.

I paused, considering what would be the best plan of attack. "Mmm...obviously, a spell of protection for the house, but I think I'll place another one here on this closet, just to be sure, and then I'll also cast a spell of illusion so this door blends into the wall. Only you and your family will know it's here."

"You can do all that?" she asked. From her expression, I could tell she was doing her best to be polite even though I was straining—for her, anyway—the bounds of credibility.

I did my best to smother a smile. After all, even though I'd taken over the *prima* position and defeated Simon Escobar, Sophia hadn't seen me in action. She didn't know what I was capable of.

"All that and more," Rafe said, stepping in for me. He'd probably guessed, and rightly, that I didn't want to defend myself too vigorously in case it sounded as though I was boasting. "Miranda's range of talents is far beyond what any of us have ever seen."

"Well, then," Sophia said, sounding resigned. She extended a hand toward the closet and the safe within. "Go ahead."

"Okay." I shut my eyes for a moment, envisioning a bubble of protection encasing this house and everyone and everything within it. Although no one could see that magical shield, I knew it was there, providing a sure defense for Sophia and her family—however many of them might still live here. I knew Tony had his own place, but he'd mentioned a sister that night we'd met at the Halloween party. Did she still live at home, or was she married already and off somewhere with her own family?

In the end, it didn't really matter all that much. As soon as anyone came into this house, they would be protected by the spell, too. Well, as long as they came here with good intentions. Someone intent on causing harm would never get past the front door.

Now that the house was protected, I shifted my focus to the closet behind that innocuous-looking door. Another magical shield, this one smaller, providing an extra layer of protection beyond the one offered by the first spell I'd cast. This one I fine-tuned slightly so that it would only allow Sophia or myself to pass it; there really wasn't any reason for anyone else in her family to go in there, anyway.

And finally, the spell of illusion. That was easy enough, because all I had to do was make it look like a plain expanse of drywall painted the same biscuit-y beige as the rest of the room. A final intention that all these spells should last until I removed the enchantment, and it was done.

When I opened my eyes, I saw Sophia standing by the spot in question along the far wall. Her hand moved along the space where the door should be, and she shook her head. "I can't even feel it."

"That's the point," I said. "You want to make

sure that no one can detect the door by touch or by sight. I've set it up so you can get in, though." I went over to her and stretched out my hand to the place where I knew the doorknob was located. "If you reach for the doorknob, it'll open for you. *Only* you, though—there's no point in showing this to anyone in your family, because I've locked down the spell so you and I are the only ones who have access. I thought that was probably best."

"Yes, neither Leo nor Noel has any reason to get in there." Sophia turned away from the door and gave me a relieved smile, some of that taut impression gone from her face now. "Thank you, Miranda."

I didn't say it was nothing, because I knew it wasn't. Those books needed to be kept safe, and now they were as unreachable as if they'd been locked up at Fort Knox. Just another part of being *prima*, although I hoped there wouldn't be any more crises until after the wedding. It wasn't so much that doing this kind of magic tired me out, only that it could be mentally exhausting to have to keep wondering what might come down the pike next.

Instead, I smiled at Sophia and told her I was happy to help, and after that Rafe and I made our goodbyes and headed out to the Jeep. By that point, December's early dusk had already fallen, so I couldn't see a lot of detail as we left the tract where Sophia's home was located and drove back down the hill a little ways. Not too far, because I could tell we'd gone barely a mile before Rafe turned onto a small road that wound through carefully manicured grounds with low landscape lighting.

"The restaurant here does sort of a Japanese version of tapas," he explained as we got out of the Wrangler. "Small plates that we're supposed to share. But not really sushi," he added quickly.

"Was I that obvious?" I asked.

A grin. "Sort of. Or maybe I just heard you thinking really loudly."

Well, Arizona wasn't exactly a hotbed for gourmet sushi, so I'd never had it. With the right recommendation, I probably would have given it a try, but it didn't seem as if that was going to be an issue here.

The restaurant was beautiful, done in a spare, elegant Japanese style with carefully cloistered booths. I doubted we had a reservation, but that didn't seem to matter, as the hostess whisked us away to a booth in a corner, and almost immediately a waiter appeared to take our drink orders.

Still smiling a little, Rafe asked for a bottle of priorat, which I'd never even heard of. The waiter nodded and disappeared, and Rafe said, "I figured you probably would rather have wine than sake."

"I don't know," I replied. "I've never had sake."

"We'll come up and try a flight sometime," he said. "But after what you just had to do at Sophia's house, I thought you might want something a little more familiar."

"Except that I don't know what a priorat even is," I pointed out.

"Spanish wine. A blend of cariñena and grenache. I think you'll like it."

I had no doubt that I would. Nodding, I looked down at the menu, and for a few minutes we went back and forth on all the options and combinations, finally deciding to start with the house-made gyoza and some miso-glazed chicken drumsticks, and then move on to steak and fries and smoked pork ribs.

It sounded like a lot of food, even though Rafe had warned me the plates would be small. After the waiter had returned with the wine and taken our orders, I took a sip of the priorat— which was amazing—and said, "Do you have any other surprises like that lurking in the wings?"

Rafe didn't ask me what I meant by "other surprises." "No," he replied. "Or at least, I hope not. I know we haven't talked much about *him*— and I completely understand why—but I think the books were the only thing that was difficult to dispose of. Louisa handled most of it...his clothing was burned, the ritual knife and candle-sticks destroyed. The only things that were left were those books, and I know we would have gotten rid of them if we could. But technically, they're the property of the de la Pazes, so our hands are tied."

For a moment, I sipped my wine and didn't say anything. I supposed I should have been glad that Louisa had stepped up and managed the disposal of Simon's effects, but I wish someone had talked to me about it. Not that I had an issue with anything they'd done, but because I was the *prima* and it was my responsibility to know these things.

Well, done was done. The books were as protected as they could be, and there hadn't been even a whisper of any other dark witches or warlocks out there—or anyone not from the Castillo clan trying to come into New Mexico— so I figured we were safe enough for now. Still, once things had settled down, I'd need to talk to Zoe, the de la Paz *prima,* and also reach out somehow to Marisol Gutierrez, the head witch of the Santiago clan. She might have disowned Simon years before, but she still deserved to know that her son was dead.

A small sigh escaped my lips, and Rafe reached across the table to take my hand. "Hey," he said. "It's going to be okay. The books are safe. We're having a nice evening out. You don't have to solve all the problems of the world in one day."

I smiled across the table at him. "I would have made a terrible poker player, wouldn't I?"

"The worst," he agreed cheerfully. "You've done your duty as *prima*. Now you get to be just Miranda for the rest of the night."

"Sounds like a plan," I said, and thought, *Here's hoping I get to be "just Miranda" for the foreseeable future....*

6

THE DAYS SPED BY AFTER THAT. NO OTHER specters from our past conflict with Simon Escobar raised their ugly heads, and so I was free to continue settling in as *prima* and making sure everything would be in order when the big day rolled around. Cat's new home got a clean bill of health from the house inspector, and so she was busy securing estimates and lining up contractors to get started with the remodel after the holidays were over.

My parents were coming for the wedding, of course, and agreed to stay through Christmas Eve —mostly because I painted such a pretty portrait of what the Canyon Road walk would be like, my mother didn't want to miss it—although they'd go home that same night so they could spend Christmas Day with their grandchildren. I supposed I couldn't ask for much more than that, since they were now having to split their time between family members in two different states. This was where their talent for teleporting would come in really handy, since at least they wouldn't have to spend hours on the road going back and forth between Jerome and Santa Fe.

At the same time, I wondered what they would do once they had grandchildren here in New Mexico. Rafe and I hadn't talked about that very much, but I knew some of his relatives—his Aunt Rosa in particular—kept looking at my waistline with a speculative eye.

As if I'd let myself get pregnant before the official wedding ceremony. I wanted to drink champagne at my reception, and besides, I didn't dare risk not fitting in my gown. Yes, I knew that a few weeks probably wouldn't make a difference, but what if I was one of those women who started to expand the second she got pregnant? That dress fit me like a glove. Even a few pounds could make all the difference in the world.

At some point, though, Rafe and I would have to discuss having children. To be honest, I didn't want to put it off for too long. Right now, there was no *prima*-in-waiting designated for the Castillo clan, and I had a gut feeling that there wouldn't be until I had a daughter of my own. I'd broached the subject of a successor with Rafe fairly early on, hoping he would have some insights about who would make a good candidate, but he didn't have any wisdom to offer, only said that while the Castillos had a lot of strong witches in the correct age bracket, none of them stood out enough for him to recommend them as my heir.

Even though I'd halfway anticipated such a response, I couldn't help but be disappointed. It would have been a relief to know there was someone standing in the wings in case anything happened to me. But I reminded myself that my mother didn't have a *prima*-in-waiting for years and years, and yet the McAllisters had thrived during that time, and no crisis had emerged to force her to make a choice. I was past my own crisis now, and I knew I needed to be patient. The universe would let me know when my heir appeared, and until then I'd just have to bide my time.

I'd been carefully watching the weather forecasts, and was worried that snow might mar my wedding day. Not that I hoped to deprive anyone of a white Christmas, but I really didn't want to dodge snowflakes as I was leaving the cathedral or going into the reception hall. Luckily, the Castillo clan's weather-workers stepped in and let me know that they'd hold back the storm for as long as they could.

"Not forever," Rafe's cousin Lina told me. She

was a pretty woman in her forties, a bit rounder than most of the Castillo women, but with charming dimples and big brown eyes. "But at least twenty-four hours. That'll bring the snow on Christmas Eve or Christmas Day, which is much better timing for everyone involved."

I thanked her, and told her to also give my thanks to the other weather workers in the clan for their assistance. Although sometimes being born into a witch family could be a real pain in the ass, there were other times when I was profoundly grateful for all the million and one things, big and small, that our magic could do for us.

Cat and I had already agreed that I'd stay with her at her Airbnb the night before the ceremony.

"That way, you won't see me until I walk down the aisle," I told Rafe one afternoon, with less than one week to go until we stood in the cathedral and exchanged vows.

He treated me to an epic eye roll. "Miranda, we've been living together for a month, and we're already legally married. Do you really think it's going to make that big a difference if I see you the day of the ceremony?"

I'd anticipated this protest, so I replied immediately. "It might. Do you really want to take any chances, especially after everything we've been through to get to this point?"

Judging by the way he just stood there, arms crossed, mouth quirked in that wry way which was peculiarly his, he didn't appear terribly impressed by my question. "I had no idea you were this superstitious."

"I'm not being superstitious," I protested. "I'm just trying to play it safe. I appreciate that you're so crazy about me that you can't bear to be apart for even one night, but—"

He didn't allow me to get any farther than that, because he came over and pulled me into his arms, then gave me a very hearty kiss. After he lifted his mouth from mine, he said, voice almost a growl, "I am crazy about you. Or maybe it's just that you make me crazy. Either way is fine by me."

Then his arms went around me again, only this time it was to lift me from where I stood in the kitchen and carry me upstairs to our bedroom, where he proceeded to show me exactly how crazy he was by making love to me for a delicious hour. Afterward, I lay in his arms, well content, listening to the beating of his heart and breathing in the enticing scent of his skin, warm and clean at the same time.

"I'm still staying with Cat," I said, and he chuckled.

"I never assumed you would do anything different."

And that was why I loved him so much. He

didn't try to change who I was, or try to make me over in the mold of the Castillo *primas*…whatever that might be. Maybe it was because he'd fought so hard for so long to avoid expectations, and therefore would never place the weight of unwanted expectation on me.

Head pillowed against his shoulder, I murmured, "I love you."

His hand passed over my hair, heavy and yet gentle at the same time. "And I love you. More than I ever thought possible. But," he added, an amused flicker in his voice, "I'll be damn glad when this wedding is over."

"Me, too," I said. That was all, though; we both knew why we needed to do this, why we had to let as many of the Castillo clan as possible see us formally married in a church. I was now their *prima,* for better or worse, and they needed to see me as Rafe's wife, not just some witch he was shacked up with.

And though it was afternoon, and we both had tasks we probably should have been attending to, we fell asleep as we held one another, as if we both wanted to make sure to cherish some of our precious alone time together. Soon enough, things would be busy and chaotic, but for now it was just the two of us, as I'd hoped it would be.

❄

Time marched on, just like it always did, and soon enough I found myself packing all the things I would need for my stay at Cat's place, including the all-important wedding gown. She came by and picked me up, since I still didn't have a car of my own, and we'd both agreed it would be better not to have Rafe come over. My parents wouldn't be arriving until the next day, since that way they only had to worry about getting a hotel room for one night.

I was a little disappointed that they wouldn't be spending much time at all in New Mexico, although I understood why they didn't want to seem as though they were intruding. The McAllisters and the Wilcoxes and the de la Pazes all roamed in and out of each other's territories without anyone raising much of an eyebrow, while the Castillos had always held themselves aloof. That situation would probably change as time went on—I intended to be a very different sort of *prima* than Genoveva Castillo had been—but even I knew that I couldn't rush things, would have to gently guide the clan into a more inclusive way of looking at their witch family neighbors.

In the meantime, I had a wedding to get through.

Cat's Airbnb was truly gorgeous, a spacious two-bedroom house only a few blocks from the large hacienda-style home where she'd grown up.

The place had been extensively updated and exquisitely furnished, with a garden that was probably beautiful in the summer.

"You sure about the winery?" I asked after she'd given me a quick tour. "I'm not sure I'd want to move out of this place."

She chuckled. "I thought about it, but the owner doesn't want to sell. He makes too much off vacation rentals. Besides, I really wanted to be away from town."

Well, she would certainly be far enough away once she was living on the former Luna Rio winery's grounds. I told myself that having her twenty minutes from me really wasn't that big a deal, but I still couldn't help but experience a small twinge of loss at the thought. Cat was the only real friend I'd made here. Rafe loved me, and his father and two other sisters had been welcoming enough, and yet I didn't really look at Cat as a sister-in-law, but instead someone to hang out with, someone to show me her favorite shops and restaurants, doing whatever she could to help me feel a bit more comfortable in my adopted city.

"You're definitely in the heart of it here," I said, doing my best to sound neutral. The winery purchase was a done deal, so I didn't see the point in giving Cat any guilt about getting away from the place where she'd been born.

"And I can't wait to see what you do with the winery."

"I can't wait, either. I wish my witchy talent was to speed up time so I could live there now instead of having to wait for months and months." She went to the refrigerator and pulled out a bottle of white wine. "A little pre-nuptial celebration?"

"A very little," I replied. "I don't want to be all puffy tomorrow."

"I highly doubt a few glasses of wine will make you puffy, but sure." After fetching a couple of wine glasses from the cupboard, she uncorked the wine and poured for both of us—fairly generous pours, enough that having one glass wouldn't be too much of a hardship.

I raised an eyebrow. "That's 'a very little'?"

"Well, it's less than two glasses, isn't it?" she replied, a glint in her dark eyes telling me that she'd guessed I would call out the way she'd poured the wine until it was a scant half inch from the lip of the glass.

"Technically."

She chuckled. "You looked like you needed it."

"Is it that obvious?"

"To most people, probably not." With the hand that held her own wine glass, she gestured toward the living room. "Let's go sit down."

We left the kitchen and went and took our seats on the living room's comfortable, nicely worn brown leather couches. A fire crackled in the hearth, because although the weather remained clear, it was quite cold, clear and bright and hard as a diamond. The work of the Castillo clan's weather witches? Probably. Now it just needed to hold for another day.

For a minute or two, we sipped wine in companionable silence. That was another thing I liked about Cat—she didn't feel the need to chatter all the time if she didn't have something important to talk about. And even though I knew this wasn't really her home, the Airbnb felt homey to me, someplace where I could relax. I still didn't feel completely at ease in the big Castillo homestead, despite having lived there for more than a month now. At some point, I supposed I would truly settle in, would stop looking over my shoulder for the ghosts of past *primas* to appear and order me, the usurper, off the premises, but for now I still felt as though I was trespassing in the big old house.

It was also good to know that we wouldn't be chasing all over the next morning, that the hairdresser and makeup artist were going to come here to polish up Cat and me. I'd decided that I didn't want to have a big procession of bridesmaids, and so Cat would be my maid of honor and only attendant, just as Tony would be Rafe's best man and we'd leave it at that. Possibly I'd ruffled a few feathers, but I didn't see the point in having a bunch of bridesmaids who weren't personal friends.

After taking another sip of wine, Cat asked, "It's really just going to be your parents tomorrow?"

"Yes," I replied. "Both my sister and brother have small children, and that's a lot of people for even my mother and father to teleport. They could've flown, I suppose, but…." I let the words trail off there. Although both Ian and Emily had told me they were proud of me, proud of who I'd become in the Castillo clan, I got the distinct impression from Emily that she was a little annoyed that I, the one who wasn't supposed to have any magic at all, had turned out to be not only a stronger witch than she was, but had also managed to become *prima* of a witch family as old and powerful as the Castillos. It probably hadn't required much of an internal struggle for her to come up with a convenient excuse as to why she couldn't travel to Santa Fe for the ceremony. I could have allowed myself to be irritated with her, but I decided it was better to let it go. Why harbor resentment over something that, in the end, was really quite trivial?

And Ian—well, his wife Mia was in the early

pukey stage of pregnancy, so I could see why neither flying nor teleportation nor a long car ride was on her list of fun things to do. I didn't mind, and I told Ian that. He sounded relieved I hadn't pressed the issue, but had instead reassured him that I totally understood why none of them were up to traveling right now.

To my relief, Cat didn't press me for a more detailed explanation of my family's disappearing act. "Well, there'll be so many Castillos there, I doubt you'll notice the absence of any McAllisters or Wilcoxes."

"Exactly," I said. "Besides, you're all my family now, too."

She smiled, but I thought I noticed something hesitant about her expression, as if she could tell I was doing my best to put a brave face on things and hide my disappointment about having so few of my Arizona family members present. Clearly changing the subject, she said, "I still can't believe you're not going on a honeymoon."

"It's all right," I told her. "Santa Fe is kind of a destination anyway, and it's not as though we could go flying off to Tahiti or something, thanks to the way we witches have to stick around our home territories. We were talking about going to Tucson or Scottsdale sometime in February or March, though, just to be someplace where it's warm and sunny."

"That's probably a good idea. It can get pretty dreary around here in late winter."

So I'd heard, which was why Rafe and I had discussed getting away to southern Arizona for a change of pace when the winter blues started to set in. I'd never been to Tucson, and while I'd spent some time in the Phoenix area, I still wasn't very familiar with it. Being able to escape there for a few days would be fun.

Unfortunately, we wouldn't be able to stay much longer than that. Being *prima* wasn't the sort of occupation that provided many vacation days.

Cat and I chatted a bit more after that, about her plans for the winery, about good places to go in New Mexico if you just wanted to get away for a few days. Once we determined we were hungry, we decided to get Indian takeout, and spent a bit of time mulling over the menu from a local place that delivered. Just common, ordinary things, with no mention of the wedding the next day. I guessed that Cat knew I was keyed up and tense, and so didn't want to rehash something that really couldn't be changed at this date anyway.

And after we'd eaten and watched a movie and decided it was time to go to bed, I surprised her by giving her a quick hug.

"What was that for?" she asked.

"Just to say thanks," I replied. "Thanks for

keeping my mind off things, thanks for letting me crash here tonight. You know."

"Then you're welcome," she said. "You'll have fun tomorrow, you really will. It's not going to be some huge production. Just a quiet ceremony, followed by a blow-out party at the reception."

"A 'quiet ceremony' with three hundred guests," I pointed out.

Not a blink as she returned, "True, but I promise that you won't have to remember all their names."

It was my turn to chuckle. "Oh, well, then it'll be a piece of cake."

"Exactly. Now, get a good night's sleep. It's insomnia that will make you puffy, not a couple glasses of wine."

"Yes, ma'am." I sent her a smile and then went into my borrowed room. It had an *en suite* bath, which meant I wouldn't have to come out again until the next morning after I'd showered and put on some comfy clothes to await the arrival of the hairdresser and the makeup artist. At the thought of those preparations, a little quiver of nervous anticipation went through me. Cat could say this wasn't a big deal, and I could try to convince myself of that same fact, but I couldn't ignore what had happened the first time we'd tried this. I couldn't forget how I'd stood on the altar at Loretto Chapel and heard those terrible words coming from Rafe's mouth. Yes, it wouldn't happen again, because Simon Escobar was dead, and his dark magic had died with him.

Still....

I shook my head as I turned down the covers on the bed. History wouldn't repeat itself. It couldn't.

All the same, I knew I wouldn't be able to relax until the ceremony was over.

7

I DIDN'T THINK I'D EVER BEEN SO GLAD TO SEE someone as I was when I turned away from the mirror in the cathedral's dressing room and saw my parents standing just inside the door, Cat behind them, quickly shutting that same door so no one could see me in my bridal splendor. Yes, Tony had sworn that he'd make sure Rafe wouldn't try to take a peek, but, considering Tony's lackadaisical attitude about most things, I wasn't sure I could trust him to keep his word.

"Miranda, you look stunning," my mother said, coming toward me with with her hands out in greeting. I took them, and felt a certain odd comfort in their familiar touch. She looked beautiful, too, with her dark hair up in a complicated knot at the back of her head, and wearing an extremely chic dark green suit and high heels. The ensemble was so out of character for her—she usually wore jeans and flowy tops in the summer, or bulky sweaters in the winter—that I knew she'd must have made a special effort to show the Castillos that the McAllisters weren't a bunch of rubes from the Arizona hills.

"You're looking pretty stunning yourself," I replied. We couldn't really hug, because I knew both of us were worried about wrinkling the silken splendor of my wedding gown, but I squeezed her fingers, taking comfort from her touch. "Where'd you get that outfit? Scottsdale?"

"How'd you know?"

"Last time I checked, I didn't see anything like that in Jerome or Sedona."

She smiled. "Well, that's true enough."

My father approached. He wore a dark gray suit with a tie patterned in gray and green, colors that suited his mossy hazel eyes. Again, completely out of character for him, since I couldn't even remember the last time I'd seen him wearing dress pants rather than jeans. "Your mother wanted to make sure we made a good impression."

"Well, I'm pretty sure you're going to do that without any problem." I went on my tiptoes and gave him the lightest of kisses on the cheek, one that left only a faint trace of lip gloss. Holding back a smile, I reached up and whisked the gloss away with my fingertips.

He touched his face where I'd kissed him. "You got it all?"

"Of course," I said, trying not to smile too much.

"We're so proud of you," my mother said then. "Overcoming a threat like the one Simon Escobar presented, becoming *prima* of the Castillos—we'd hoped for great things for you, but I don't think either your father or I ever expected quite this much."

A little rush of warmth went through me. Of course I knew my parents loved me, but still, it was good to hear that they also took some pride in my accomplishments, especially since it hadn't been so very long ago when I hadn't exactly showed much promise in the magic department. "Well, I hope that was the end of it," I replied. "I think we've all had enough excitement to last us for a while."

"A wedding is also exciting," my mother pointed out. "At least, I hope you think it is."

This certainly wasn't the time to point out the misgivings I'd been experiencing, so all I could do was lift my shoulders and say, "I do. But this is really more for the clan than it is for Rafe and me. What I'm really looking forward to is the reception."

Both my parents chuckled at that remark, and Cat stepped forward and said, "We're getting close to the time for the ceremony. Do you want me to show you where you need to be?" Because of course my father would be walking me down the aisle this time, and my mother would sit in the front pew. Once again, I wondered if things might have been different if they'd been present for that first wedding ceremony, whether they would have detected the terrible spell Simon had cast on Rafe. I'd never know the answer, and in the end, maybe it was better this way. The love Rafe and I shared was much stronger because of how we'd had to fight for it.

"It's all right, Cat," my father said. "We know where we need to go. Besides, you're the maid of honor—you need to stay here with Miranda." He paused, then glanced over at me. "I'll see you in a few minutes."

I smiled at him, and both he and my mother left the dressing room. Cat closed the door, then turned toward me, one eyebrow lifted in that ironic way she shared with her brother.

"You could have told me your father was such a hottie."

"He's twenty-five years older than you are," I pointed out. "And happily married."

"Yes, I can see that, thank you very much." She tilted her head so the little diamond drops she wore in her ears twinkled in the light from the clerestory windows high above us. "It's not like I was going to go after him or something. I was just making a statement of fact." A little pause, and an impish light entered her dark eyes. "Maybe that's been my problem all along. Maybe I just like older men better."

"Possibly," I said. For her sake, I kind of hoped not. It was very rare to find an unmarried warlock in his thirties, or older. "We can talk about that later, after the wedding."

"Right." A glance up at the clock that hung on the far wall of the dressing room, and she said, "Well, time to go. Let's get you properly married."

"I *am* properly married," I protested, but I dutifully followed her out of the room and down the hallway that led to the chapel itself. As we drew closer, I could hear soft organ music playing, although I couldn't make out the tune. Something traditional, probably; the Castillos were all about tradition, whereas we McAllisters were the exact opposite.

My father was waiting in the vestibule; he held out his arm to me as the music transitioned to Pachelbel's *Canon*. I hadn't wanted to walk down the aisle to the wedding march, just because it always felt a little too loud and bombastic to me. Luckily, Pachelbel was orthodox enough that I didn't get a peep of protest over the substitution, not even from Rafe's Aunt Rosa.

Cat went ahead of us, walking serenely down

the aisle in her blush-pink bridesmaid's gown, dark head held high. The color suited her, brought a warmth to her olive skin, although I didn't think I'd really seen her wear it much before this. As I watched her go, I wondered if I'd done the right thing by having only a maid-of-honor and no other attendants, since she did look rather small in contrast to the chapel's lofty ceilings.

Well, it couldn't be helped now. Anyway, I didn't have time to worry about those kinds of details, because it was now my turn to emerge from the vestibule and walk down the aisle. My father's arm supported me, allowed me to carry my head just as high as Cat had. The last time I'd done this, Rafe's father Eduardo had held my arm, and I'd been grateful for his presence. Still, it wasn't the same as having my own father next to me, or knowing that my mother waited in the front pew.

Would things have turned out differently if they'd been present at the first ceremony? Could they, with the strength of their combined powers, have detected Simon's dark magic working on Rafe and figured out a way to block it or stop it somehow?

Possibly. I'd never know for sure, though, and at this point, did it really matter? When you got right down to it, Simon's spell had backfired on him, because in a strange, terrible way, what he'd done to Rafe and me had only drawn us closer in the end, had allowed us to realize how much we truly did care for one another. This second ceremony would have so much more meaning to us because of that.

And there Rafe was, standing on the altar next to his cousin Tony, smiling down at me, his eyes full of admiration as he caught his first glimpse of me in my wedding gown. I'd heard the murmurs of appreciation while I walked down the aisle, but it was really Rafe's approval I wanted.

A gentle touch on my arm, and then my father quietly let go so he could sit down next to my mother and I could ascend the altar steps to stand next to Rafe. As I took my place next to him, he leaned in and murmured, "You are the most beautiful woman I've ever seen."

A pleased flush rose to my cheeks, but all I could do was send him a quick smile, since the priest had already begun the ceremony.

"Dearly beloved, we are gathered here together...."

Thank the Goddess that the ceremony was being conducted in English, not Latin. Most Catholic churches had long ago abandoned the use of the dead language, but, as I'd previously noted, the Castillos tended to stick to the traditional, and Santa Fe itself was much the same way, for all its surface vibe of being a funky artists' haven. In this instance, though, Rafe had prevailed, which meant I didn't have to worry about not understanding what was going on during my own wedding.

When the time came, he said solemnly, "With this ring, I thee wed," and slipped the band of diamonds onto my left hand. I hadn't wanted a big ostentatious solitaire, but we'd found a local jeweler who created lovely, intricate designs, and the two-tone band of delicate scrolls set with tiny winking diamonds was just what I wanted. The ring felt at home on my finger, as though it had always been intended to rest there.

I did the same with Rafe, placing the brushed-titanium band we'd chosen on his ring finger. His hand shook a little, and I realized how important this had been to him as well, despite the attitude he'd adopted of casual nonchalance when it came to this second ceremony of ours. Now we really did feel married, even though we'd been husband and wife in the eyes of the state of New Mexico for a month.

"You may kiss the bride," the priest said, and here was the magic moment, the touch of Rafe's lips against mine, the faint rustle of his expensive suit as he pulled me close and held me for a long moment. The thrill that went through me told me that yes, I was very happy to now be Miranda Castillo, a permanent part of the family.

The organist started to play the traditional processional, and Rafe and I turned toward our watching family members so they could all stand and applaud. I caught a glimpse of my mother in the first row, tears gleaming in the green eyes that were so like mine, my father looking a bit damp-eyed as well next to her, and then it was all a blur as we walked down the aisle, hand in hand, finally being able to enjoy the moment that Simon Escobar had tried to steal from us.

It was then that I realized he truly was gone, no longer had any power to disrupt our lives. I'd been conjuring images of him as some sort of bogeyman who could return from the grave and continue to create havoc, but those were only my own fears talking. For all Simon's amazing gifts, he'd still just been a mortal man, one who had no more control over life and death than any of the rest of us did. It was time to leave him in the past.

As much as I wanted to head over to the reception site and pop the champagne, we still had to pause here at the cathedral for a while so the photographer could get the requisite shots, some of Rafe and me, some with our small wedding party, others with my parents and Eduardo. As that photo was taken, I reached over and squeezed Rafe's hand, doing my best to let him know how sorry I was that his mother couldn't be here with us on this happy day.

He didn't speak, but an answering warmth in his eyes told me that he understood. I'd worried a bit about his apparent lack of mourning for Genoveva, although I'd done my best to tell myself that everyone grieved in their own way, and Rafe certainly wasn't the type to indulge in showy displays of sorrow. No, it was the little things, like the way he'd pause when he passed by the picture of his family that sat on the large mantel in the living room, or the way he talked about the gardens and how much his mother had loved them. His wasn't a hard heart, but a quiet one, and I knew I had to let himself progress through his grieving on his own timetable and in a manner that felt comfortable for him.

At last, though, the photographer determined that he had enough shots he could use, and we were set free to go enjoy ourselves at the reception. An elegant self-driving limo whisked Rafe and me away to the restaurant, and the rest of the wedding party followed. The guests had preceded us, and so they'd had a good forty-five minutes to eat and drink while the pictures were being taken.

It was no surprise to me that Tony made a beeline for the bar. From across the room, I thought I saw his mother send him a disapproving look as he ordered a martini for himself, but he seemed prepared to ignore her. And really, it wasn't as though he had any official duties to manage until the time came to give the toast.

For myself, after standing in heels for more than an hour, I was all too happy to have Rafe guide me to the head table so I could sit down. He went to fetch us some champagne, giving me a chance to finally take in my surroundings. Although Cat and I had selected the decorations together, I hadn't been involved in putting them up, and so the fairytale winter wonderland I saw now was enough to take my breath away. Swags of tulle with fairy lights glimmering behind them decorated the ceiling, and more lights glittered from the bare white-painted trees that stood like sentinels along the walls. Each centerpiece was a large glass column with flowers and leaves submerged in water, and little battery-powered lights gleaming from within the underwater flora.

All taken together, the transformed dining area at Eduardo's restaurant was more beautiful than I could have imagined, and tears of happiness pricked at my eyes as I looked at the result of Cat's hard work—and the hard work of the Castillo cousins she'd drafted to assist in decorating the hall. However, I blinked those tears back as Rafe approached, a glass of champagne in each hand. The last thing I wanted was for him to think that I was unhappy in any way. No, I was just the opposite.

"It looks gorgeous," I told him as he handed a champagne flute to me. "Do I want to know how long all this took?"

"Just an afternoon, according to Cat," Rafe replied. "A lot of people pitched in to help, and then the florist handled the final setup with the table arrangements."

"Where is Cat, anyway?" I asked. I scanned the crowd, but I didn't see anyone wearing a long, blush-colored dress.

Rafe appeared to look over the crowd as well, then nodded. "She's over by the door, talking to your parents."

I glanced in that direction. Sure enough, the three of them stood by the door that led out into the restaurant proper, having what looked like an animated conversation. About what, I had no idea, although I hoped that Cat hadn't taken it into her head to try flirting with my father. Most likely, my parents would find such an attempt amusing more than anything else, but still....

Whatever the discussion had been about, it didn't seem to last long. Cat made some kind of comment and headed over toward the bar, while my parents went in the opposite direction, toward the spot where Eduardo and Louisa and Louisa's husband Oscar stood talking.

"They all look like they're having a good time," I said.

"Of course they are." Rafe set his champagne flute down on the table and reached over to trace a gentle finger over my forearm. It was the softest of touches, but still enough to send a flicker of desire through me...even though we were surrounded by family members. "They just saw their daughter get married."

"I was talking about Cat and your family, too."

"Well, same thing, basically. Now we can all relax and enjoy ourselves, you know?"

Looking out at the Castillos gathered there, at my own parents, I thought I did know. There were times when we'd all thought this day would never arrive. Now was the time to take a breath, to realize there wasn't anything or anyone to get in the way of our happy future.

The evening did feel like a dream—that first glass of champagne was followed by another, and then some wonderful red wine to go with the Beef Wellington served as the main course. Then more champagne, and Tony standing up to make the toast. The Goddess only knew how many drinks he'd had by that point, although he seemed steady enough as he raised his champagne flute.

"I thought about making a big fancy speech," he said. "But I guessed you all didn't want to sit here and listen to me drone on for ten minutes. All I wanted to say really boiled down to this, anyway—Rafe and Miranda are proof that you need to fight for what you want. They never gave up on each other, or this clan, no matter how badly things seemed to be going. And now they're together, and all you have to do is look at them together to know how happy they are. I hope"—Tony paused there, and seemed to ponder whether he wanted to continue the sentence or not. Apparently, he decided to do so, because he finished by saying, "I hope one day I can love someone the way they love each other. Congratulations!"

From all around the room came echoes of, "Congratulations!," and everyone raised their champagne glass as well and took a hearty swallow. I drank, too, mostly because Tony's words had made those tears return to my eyes, and I thought the best way to banish them was to have some of what my parents had always jokingly referred to as "fizzy lifting drinks."

But there wasn't much time to get too misty, because after that was a dance, Rafe holding me close, the strength of his arms telling me that he'd always be my champion—even though he knew I could take care of myself—and then the cutting off the cake, and finally, finally, an escape to the limo, which brought us home.

The soft glow of the lights from the Christmas tree greeted us; Rafe must have made sure they were plugged in before he left for the cathedral. I loved that he'd done that, had wanted to have me come home to that delicate reminder of the season. After he carried me over the threshold—and I once again protested that he really didn't need to do that—he kissed me under the mistletoe which hung from the ceiling in the foyer.

"Welcome home, Mrs. Castillo," he said.

I arched an eyebrow at him. "I don't recall telling you that I was going to change my name."

He grinned at me. "I really don't care one way or another…but since you're the *prima* of the clan, it might be a good idea."

True enough. Besides, I was already a hyphenate—my birth certificate said "Miranda Marie McAllister-Wilcox," which was enough of a mouthful. I didn't see how I could get away with adding another last name to that over-extended string of words.

"You're right, of course. Well, then, Mr. Castillo…why don't you take me upstairs and make it worth my while for me to change my last name?"

"With pleasure." Once again, he scooped me up in his arms, then ascended the wide staircase that led to the second floor. A bit of fumbling with the buttons on the back of my dress, and then I was free of the heavy satin creation.

I wouldn't let it tumble to the floor, however.

Standing there in my bustier and panties and thigh-highs, I grabbed the gown and then carefully laid it over the back of a nearby chair. While I was busy with that task, Rafe summoned a fire to the hearth, then stood there and watched me, an appreciative gleam in his eyes.

"What are you looking at?" I asked.

"You," he said simply. "Earlier, I told you that you were the most beautiful woman I'd ever seen. Now I'm wondering whether I was underestimating you."

"I doubt it," I said, a flush spreading over my face. While I enjoyed his admiration, I'd never been very good about accepting compliments.

"Oh, I know it."

He came to me and kissed me again, and I pulled at his tie, freeing it from around his neck. Soon enough, his suit coat, shirt, pants, and socks landed in an unceremonious pile near the foot of the bed, since clearly he didn't care much about their fate.

Not that I was thinking about our clothes by that point. Our bodies were pressed together, our mouths locked, and his fingers slipped into me even as I wrapped my hand around his shaft, feeling how hard he was already. By this point, we both knew how much the other person could take before the climax hit; I released my grasp on him at the same time he pushed me down onto the covers, plunging into me, the two of us moving as one, bringing the other closer, closer....

Rafe came first, but barely...or maybe it was the sensation of him reaching orgasm that pushed me over the edge, my entire body shuddering with release, my legs wrapped around him to hold him in for just a bit longer, so I might extend this moment, this timeless expanse where our hearts seemed to beat as one and nothing else in the universe really mattered all that much.

At last, though, we pulled apart, but not for very long. Within the next moment, he was holding me close, my head pillowed on the firm muscles of his chest. This wasn't my first time with him, of course, but it still felt that way.

And somehow I knew it always would.

8

THE NIGHT AIR WAS BRISK AND COLD AGAINST my face as we all emerged from our dinner at Geronimo—Rafe and me, Eduardo, Cat, my parents. Rafe's sisters Louisa and Malena and their families had been invited as well, but they'd declined, saying it would be too late an evening for their little ones.

Just as well, since keeping even six of us together in the Christmas Eve crowds on Canyon Road was difficult enough. Cat had tried to give me an idea of what this particular Santa Fe tradition was like, but her words really hadn't prepared me for the masses of humanity that crowded every nook and cranny of the usually tranquil street. Moms and dads pushing strollers. People with their dogs, some on leashes, the smaller ones cradled in their owners' arms or even riding in a backpack. Little children laughing and running from bonfire to bonfire.

For someone who'd never experienced such a thing before, it was all a little overwhelming. I clung to Rafe's hand and strained to hear what my parents were saying to Eduardo and Cat. It sounded as though they were talking about Jerome's tradition of "lighting up the mountain," which basically meant everyone decorating their homes and shops within an inch of their lives, and turning on all the holiday lights the first Saturday after Thanksgiving. Usually, the choir from Mingus High would sing, and everyone would hang out near the steps across the street from the Spirit Room, but that quiet gathering didn't bear much of a resemblance to the rowdy celebration here on Canyon Road.

I could tell my parents were enjoying themselves, though, and it was fun to thread our way through the various galleries, especially since I hadn't yet had much of a chance to explore the shops here, despite living so close by. And I loved the little group of singers who stood on a balcony above the street, so that it sounded as if the lilting notes of "Bring a Torch, Jeannette, Isabella" were drifting down to us from heaven itself.

And suddenly, that wasn't the only thing falling down on Canyon Road from somewhere above. As we'd walked over to the restaurant earlier, I'd noticed how heavy and lowering the clouds had been, but I couldn't be sure if the weather-workers' spells were still holding back the storm or not. Now, though, tiny, airy flakes began to fall, not heavily, but like little swirling bits of the finest down. They didn't seem ready to stick to anything yet, but rather disappeared as soon as they touched the ground, the trees, and even the coats and jackets we wore.

Still, I heard a delighted "oh!" sweep through the gathered throng, and for a moment, everyone was still, the crowd's collective gaze tilted upward to the sky.

"It's beautiful," my mother murmured. She was standing next to my father, her head pillowed on his shoulder.

"It's a good omen," Eduardo said. "We haven't had snow on Christmas Eve for many years now."

"What does it predict?" I asked.

He smiled down at me, dark eyes crinkling at the corners. "It means good luck and prosperity for the year to come."

"We could definitely use some luck after the past few months," Cat remarked. She held out one gloved hand and watched as the delicate little flakes settled on her palm and then disappeared.

No one could argue with that comment. Yes, we'd come out the other side of our fight with Simon Escobar and emerged victorious, but that battle had still taken its toll, had cost the Castillos their *prima* and inflicted far too much pain and suffering on those who'd been lucky enough to survive.

I thought of the books of dark magic that Rafe's cousin Sophia had hidden in her house, and wondered whether the safeguards I'd put in place would be enough. They had to be. I was *prima* now, and it was my responsibility to make sure I kept the clan safe.

The carolers on their balcony began to quietly sing "Silent Night," and, to my surprise, those gathered around and watching the snow fall began to sing along. Even Rafe, whose fine tenor also took me by surprise. I'd never been much of a singer, but I could carry a tune…barely…and so I held on to his hand and joined in as well, the notes of the old, old tune floating on the cold night air. And when we were done, everyone stood quietly for a moment, as though they didn't want to break the spell of this snowy Christmas Eve.

But then people began to move, and talk in their little groups, and some of the noise and chatter returned to Canyon Road. I'd never look at it quite the same way, though, because I knew it had its own magic, something quite separate from the kind of magic that flowed in my veins.

"Well," my father said, "I don't know if we'll be able to top that experience. It's getting late, anyway, so I think it's time to head back to Jerome."

"Discreetly," my mother added, a small smile quirking the corners of her mouth. "We'll find a quiet corner where we can disappear without anyone noticing."

Even though I'd known they hadn't planned to stay after this evening, I couldn't quite hold back the pang of disappointment that went through me. They were right—it was getting late, and yet I wished I could make this evening last forever.

But I told myself that I needed to be a grown-up and not try to urge them to stay any longer. They had obligations back in Arizona. I should be glad that they'd been here to see me get married to Rafe, had been able to spend Christmas Eve with me.

I hugged them both and wished them a happy holiday, then stepped away so my mother could give Rafe a quick embrace. He looked a little startled, but then managed a smile and said he was very glad that we'd been able to spend this time together.

Eduardo and Cat chimed in, saying that they were happy we'd all been able to be together for the wedding and the holiday, and then my parents slipped through the crowd and disappeared into a narrow alley between two galleries. No sign to show that they'd teleported away once they were hidden from view, but I still knew they were gone.

The snow had continued to fall, but now it was growing thicker, the wind picking up. Even though I wore a warm coat and gloves and a knit cap on my head, I could tell it wouldn't be comfortable to stand out here much longer.

"We should probably head back to the house," Eduardo said, and no one tried to contradict him.

The crowds were beginning to disperse, too, everyone heading toward the base of Canyon Road and the streets and parking lots where they'd left their cars. We didn't have nearly as far to go, since all we had to do was cut across Gonzales Road and walk a few blocks to reach the big house where Rafe and I now lived.

A short pause on the covered front porch so we could knock the snow off our boots and jackets, and then we all went inside. The Christmas tree glimmered from the living room, and the air was scented with cinnamon and cloves, thanks to the potpourri I'd put out earlier that day.

"I can make some coffee," I suggested, but Eduardo shook his head.

"Thank you for the offer, but I don't drink coffee in the evening." He paused and looked over at his daughter. "But if Cat would like some…."

"No, that's all right," she said immediately. "It would only keep me up, too. Besides," she went on, "you're going to be cooking all day for us tomorrow. You don't need us sticking around until all hours tonight."

That was true enough; the goose for next day's Christmas dinner was already soaking in a brine solution, and the refrigerator was packed with all the items I'd bought to create the various side dishes and desserts that would accompany the goose. Rafe had teased me about going overboard with the whole thing, but I wanted to make sure Eduardo and Cat got a proper holiday meal.

Still, I thought I should attempt at least a token protest. "It's really no trouble—"

"We're fine," she said gently. "Tomorrow at three, right?"

"Right," I replied, admitting defeat.

Rafe and I gave the two of them goodnight hugs, and then they were hurrying down the front steps and through the garden to the driveway, which was where Eduardo had left his car parked. After he shut the door, Rafe gave me an inquiring look.

"Are you okay?"

"Why wouldn't I be?" I responded...although I knew what he'd really been asking.

"I'm sorry your parents won't be here for Christmas dinner tomorrow."

"It's all right," I told him...and then I realized it really was. This was my home now, and

Eduardo and Cat my family. Of course, I hoped my parents would come back to visit soon, and I assumed Rafe and I would go to Jerome in the not-too-distant future, but my place was here—here in Santa Fe, with the man I loved at my side.

I reached out and took his hand, then stood on my tiptoes so I could kiss him on the cheek.

"You're all I want for Christmas, Rafe," I said. "You, and your family, and my life here."

A smile touched his lips, and he pulled me to him, his embrace a homecoming.

Yes, I truly had come home.

The Witches of Canyon Road will continue with Cat's story in *Demon Born,* due out in January 2019.

ALSO BY CHRISTINE POPE

THE WITCHES OF CANYON ROAD

(Paranormal Romance)

Hidden Gifts

Darker Paths

Mysterious Ways

A Canyon Road Christmas (November 2018)

Demon Born (January 2019)

THE WITCHES OF CLEOPATRA HILL*

(Paranormal Romance)

Darkangel

Darknight

Darkmoon

Sympathetic Magic

Protector

Spellbound

A Cleopatra Hill Christmas

Impractical Magic

Strange Magic

The Arrangement

Defender

Bad Blood

Deep Magic

Darktide

Books 1-3 and Books 4-6 of this series are also available in two separate omnibus editions at special boxed set prices. Chronicles of Cleopatra Hill includes the series' two "back in time" novellas, *Bad Blood* and *The Arrangement*.

THE DJINN WARS*

(Paranormal Romance)

Chosen

Taken

Fallen

Broken

Forsaken

Forbidden

Awoken

Illuminated

Books 1-3 and Books 4-6 of this series are also

available in two separate omnibus editions at special
boxed set prices!

DJINN DOMINION*

(Paranormal Romance)

Stolen

Forgotten

Driven

THE WATCHERS TRILOGY*

(Paranormal Romance)

Falling Dark

Dead of Night

Rising Dawn

THE SEDONA FILES*

(Paranormal Romance)

Bad Vibrations

Desert Hearts

Angel Fire

Star Crossed

Falling Angels

Enemy Mine

Get the first three books of this series in an omnibus edition, or read the complete six-book series in one super-low-priced boxed set!

TALES OF THE LATTER KINGDOMS

(Fantasy Romance)

All Fall Down

Dragon Rose

Binding Spell

Ashes of Roses

One Thousand Nights

Threads of Gold

The Wolf of Harrow Hall

Moon Dance

The Song of the Thrush

Snow Fall (first half of 2019)

Books 1-3 and Books 4-6 of this series are also available in two separate omnibus editions at special boxed set prices.

THE GAIAN CONSORTIUM SERIES

(Science Fiction Romance)

Beast (free prequel novella)

Blood Will Tell

Breath of Life

The Gaia Gambit

The Mandala Maneuver

The Titan Trap

The Zhore Deception

The Refugee Ruse

Books 1-3 of this series are also available in an omnibus edition at a special boxed set price!

* Indicates a completed series

STANDALONE TITLES

Hearts on Fire

Sympathy for the Devil

Taking Dictation

Night Music

Golden Heart

ABOUT THE AUTHOR

USA Today bestselling author Christine Pope has been writing stories ever since she commandeered her family's Smith-Corona typewriter back in grade school. Her work includes paranormal romance, fantasy romance, and science fiction/space opera romance. She makes her home in Sedona, Arizona.

Don't miss out on any of Christine's new releases —sign up for her newsletter today!

Christine Pope on the Web:
www.christinepope.com

www.ingramcontent.com/pod-product-compliance
Lightning Source LLC
Chambersburg PA
CBHW030234180626
46810CB00008B/3123